The McKenna Legacy...
A Legacy of Love

To my darling grandchildren,

I leave you my love and more. Within thirty-three days of your thirty-third birthday—enough time to know what you are about—you will have in your grasp a legacy of which your dreams are made. Dreams are not always tangible things, but more often are born in the heart. Act selflessly in another's behalf, and my legacy will be yours.

Your loving grandmother,
Moira McKenna

P.S. Use any other inheritance from me wisely and only for good, lest you destroy yourself or those you love.

Dear Harlequin Intrigue Reader,

The summer is here and we've got plenty of scorching suspense and smoldering romance for your reading pleasure. Starting with a couple of your favorite Harlequin Intrigue veterans...

Patricia Rosemoor winds up the reprisal of THE McKENNA LEGACY with *Cowboy Protector*. Yet another of Moira McKenna's kin feels the force of what real love can do if you're open to it. And not to be outdone, Rebecca York celebrates a silver anniversary with the twenty-fifth title in her popular 43 LIGHT STREET series. *From the Shadows* is one more fabulous mystery coupled with a steamy romance. Prepare yourself for a super surprise ending with this one!

THE CARRADIGNES come to Harlequin Intrigue this month. *The Duke's Covert Mission* by Julie Miller is a souped-up Cinderella story that will leave you breathless for sure. This brawny duke doesn't pull up in a horse-drawn carriage. He relies on a nondescript sedan with unmarked plates instead. But I assure you he's got all the breeding of the most regal royalty when it counts.

Finally, Charlotte Douglas brings you *Montana Secrets*, an emotional secret-baby story set in the Big Sky state. I dare you not to fall head over heels in love with this hidden-identity hero.

So grab the sunblock and stuff all four titles into your beach bag.

Happy reading!

Sincerely,

Denise O'Sullivan
Associate Senior Editor
Harlequin Intrigue

COWBOY PROTECTOR
PATRICIA ROSEMOOR

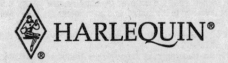

TORONTO • NEW YORK • LONDON
AMSTERDAM • PARIS • SYDNEY • HAMBURG
STOCKHOLM • ATHENS • TOKYO • MILAN • MADRID
PRAGUE • WARSAW • BUDAPEST • AUCKLAND

ISBN 0-373-22665-9

COWBOY PROTECTOR

Visit us at www.eHarlequin.com

Printed in U.S.A.

ABOUT THE AUTHOR

To research her novels, Patricia Rosemoor is willing to swim with dolphins, round up mustangs or howl with wolves…"Whatever it takes to write a credible tale." She's the author of contemporary, historical and paranormal romances, but her first love has always been romantic suspense. She won both a *Romantic Times* Career Achievement Award in Series Romantic Suspense and a Reviewer's Choice Award for one of her Harlequin Intrigue novels. She's written more than thirty Harlequin Intrigue books and is now writing for Harlequin Blaze. She lives in Chicago with her husband, Edward, and their three cats.

She would love to know what you think of this story. Write to Patricia Rosemoor at P.O. Box 578297, Chicago, IL 60657-8297 or via e-mail at Patricia@PatriciaRosemoor.com, and visit her Web site at http://PatriciaRosemoor.com.

Books by Patricia Rosemoor

Descendants of MOIRA KELLY McKENNA

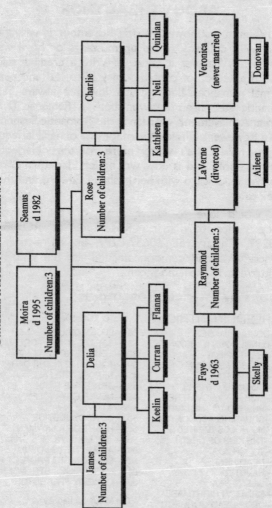

CAST OF CHARACTERS

Neil McKenna Farrell—The rancher never believed in the McKenna legacy until a hostage situation created an unbreakable bond between him and pretty Annabeth Caldwell. Can he keep her safe from harm…and his heart?

Annabeth Caldwell—The rodeo worker was the only one who saw one of the thieves' faces, but should she entrust her safety to a cowboy who won't take no for an answer?

Nickels—The leader of the hostage takers was prepared to kill to protect himself, but is he the real menace to Annabeth?

Peter Telek—The rodeo official seems really upset about Annabeth's brushes with danger. Is that because she's still alive?

Lloyd Wainwright—The contractor couldn't account for missing stock. How closely are his financial interests tied up with the rodeo?

Alderman Salvador Lujan—The local politician barely escaped from the hostage situation alive. But is his public outrage at the incident and misdirected anger at Annabeth just a cover-up?

Thanks to Michael Black, writer and police officer, for his generous help in providing me with background material. Michael—I always know I can count on your for ideas on how the authorities would handle things.

Prologue

The late-summer sun blazed down on Chicago's stifling lakefront, careless of the opening of City Slickers Rodeo Days. The crowd of several hundred thousand and growing wandered the festival grounds in a humid daze.

"Perfect," he growled, taking it all in.

Families shoulder to shoulder pushing into the arena…kids whining for pony rides…teens grumbling about two country-music stages and no hip-hop. And all of them too close to heat exhaustion to be observant.

"No one is paying us any mind," he told his cohorts. They had snaked together from three different directions to converge on the temporary building that housed the rodeo bank. He'd already taken care of the guard. "They're all drowning in their own sweat."

"Yeah, them and me."

"When we're through here," the bigger of his men said, "maybe we can go for a dip in the lake."

He glared at the two dim bulbs who made up his gang. They looked ridiculous in those getups—cowboy gear, including oversize Stetsons that shadowed their faces. But they blended with the rodeo personnel and contestants, and that was the idea. Anyone looking at them would think they were in costume, right down to the holsters hanging low on their hips.

Little would observers figure that the leather-cradled revolvers were loaded with deadly shot. He slipped his piece from its holster and slid it behind the saddlebags draped over his shoulder.

Backing toward the door to the bank office, he growled, "Let's do it!" He lifted the bandanna over his nose and unlocked the door with the keys he'd taken off the guard they'd knocked down a few minutes before.

Faces masked, guns drawn, they shoved their way in like a wedge. He stopped several feet in front of the door, while the boys fanned out, one on either side.

"What do you guys think you're doing?" the pretty young woman inside asked with a giggle.

"Robbing you, Blondie." He threw the leather saddlebags at her. "Fill them up. Twenties and bigger bills. No small stuff. Takes up too much room."

The middle-aged man on the other side of the room blustered, "You can't be serious!"

He gave the man a steely-eyed glare. "You don't want to bet on that."

To emphasize his seriousness, he raised his gun and aimed square between the man's eyes.

"All right, all right," the man said, his balding head blossoming red.

He could smell fear a dozen yards away, and Old

Baldy stank of it. He didn't think they were going to get any trouble from him.

Indeed, while Blondie emptied the box in the counter drawer, Old Baldy worked on the safe with a gun pointed at his head. Sweat rolled down the man's face and his hand shook as if palsied, but he managed to get the safe open.

"Pass the saddlebags," he said. And when the man didn't work quickly enough—those damn hands wouldn't stop shaking—he snapped, "You, get away from the safe!" He worried that someone would realize the guard wasn't at his station outside and come to investigate. "We'll take it from here."

Old Baldy stepped back and the work went quicker.

A few minutes later the safe was empty and the bags bulging. He heaved a sigh of relief.

He was saying, "I want to thank you for your cooperation," when he realized Old Baldy was surreptitiously probing his hand under the counter.

A blasted alarm!

Flying across the room, he butted the man across the face with his gun, but something told him the damage was already done. No noise split the air, but no doubt the alarm the idiot had triggered was silent.

Trying not to panic, he ordered, "Let's get out of here! Now!"

Chapter One

Neil McKenna Farrell entered barn one at half past noon, right after participating in the City Slickers Rodeo Days parade down Lake Shore Drive.

That had been the oddest experience—sitting atop a horse with Lake Michigan on one side, the Museum Campus straight ahead and the rodeo grounds on the other side, with the city office buildings scraping the sky beyond. He'd never before participated in a rodeo in a major city east of the Mississippi. First time for everything, he guessed. But when the opening ceremonies had begun in the arena, he'd quietly taken his leave. No need for him to be there. He simply wasn't and never would be a showman.

So here he was in the calf barn, looking for pen number three. Usually the calves would be rounded up together in one big pen—and that would be outside. But that was probably against city code, he guessed. And here they were split up into a half-dozen pens, probably someone's idea of a way to control them more easily.

Only, pen number three was empty.

So where the hell was Casper, the calf he was supposed to rope later that afternoon?

"Hey, anyone here?" he called out.

No answer.

But rustling sounds and grunting from the rear of the temporary barn caught his attention, so he headed in that direction, passing dozens of calves huddled together in groups. Most were either dozing or munching away on feed. Only a few critters were interested enough in his presence to follow him with liquid brown eyes.

He stopped yards short of the feed supply and took a moment to inspect a finely shaped rear sticking up in the air before clearing his throat.

"Excuse me, ma'am."

The woman fighting with the too-large-for-her bag of feed whipped around and lost her balance, landing square on that fine rear he'd been admiring.

"Whoa!" she croaked. "You scared the daylights out of me."

She didn't look too settled now, so Neil spread his hands where she could see them and said, "Sorry, ma'am, I'm harmless, honest."

"Right."

She was comely, with soft curves and long wheat-colored hair tied up in a ponytail away from her heart-shaped face. But her pleasant features were, at the moment, drawn into a frown aimed straight at him. Pushing herself up from the ground, she dusted off the back of her jeans, the tempting soft flesh there urging him to volunteer to help.

Instead, he took the smart route and shoved both

hands into his jeans pockets before he got himself into big trouble. He was here to rodeo not to womanize. Still, he wouldn't be human if he didn't notice that single trickle of sweat running down from her long throat and into the crevice of flesh peeking above her bright yellow T-shirt.

"You're working with the stock, right?" he asked, his mouth suddenly dry. "I mean, you're an employee?"

"No," she said, wiping sweat from her forehead with the back of her work glove. "I just like to roll around in the barn and get filthy."

"No need to be facetious."

That's when he noted the employee tag—big as life on her well-endowed chest—that declared her to be rodeo employee Annabeth Caldwell.

"Sorry, Annabeth, didn't see your identification."

She shrugged and said, "Look, we're shorthanded 'cause a guy didn't show this morning, so I'm real busy."

To prove it, she hauled up that feed bag that had been thwarting her. Neil didn't hesitate to lend a hand this time. He grabbed the low end and took half the weight. Then he helped her set the feed in a nearby wheelbarrow.

She gave him a considering look, a small frown puzzling her pretty blue eyes as if she couldn't figure out why he'd bothered. "Thanks, but you didn't need to do that. I'm stronger than I look."

He didn't doubt it, but what he said was, "My pleasure."

"My job," Annabeth countered.

As if to prove it, she moved the wheelbarrow to the closest pen, opened the bag and emptied it into a feeder, all with no help from him.

When she finished, she faced him, her expression soft. Open. And then she seemed to catch herself, as if she remembered she wasn't supposed to get cozy with a cowpoke.

"If you need something, mister, spit it out."

"Neil Farrell. And I need to see my calf."

"Your *personal* calf? As far as I know, Lloyd Wainwright owns all the stock used in this rodeo."

"The one I'm going to rope this afternoon," he said for clarification.

"What?" Her eyebrows arched and she suddenly sounded amused. "You have to practice?"

His turn to narrow his gaze on her. "I just want to check him out. Size him up. As a competitor, I mean."

"Yeah, some little calf is a real competitor to a full-grown man with a noosed rope and a horse."

Taking umbrage at her sarcasm, Neil drew himself to his full six feet, topping her by three or four inches.

"Calf roping is a time-honored cowboy tradition, a skill that still needs practice," he told her. "Every summer, back in South Dakota on the family ranch, we round up the new calves, rope and truss them for branding and vetting. So, you see, the calf-roping competition is actually a natural extension of ranch life."

Not to mention that competing in the timed rodeo competition was Neil's only hobby.

A weekend away from the ranch here and there

gave him much-needed relief from the pressures of a job that seemed to be getting harder and was, for sure, less feasible economically than when he had taken the reins from his father. And his parents had given him this particular weekend as a present for his birthday—his thirty-third. He'd be celebrating with his Mc-Kenna cousins later.

"Chicago isn't exactly ranching country, now, is it," Annabeth said, removing the gloves and sticking them in her jeans pocket.

"But that doesn't mean city people aren't interested in getting a taste of a different way of life," he countered.

She shrugged. "Obviously, or City Slickers Rodeo Days wouldn't be in progress."

"If you have something against rodeoing," Neil said quietly, "what are you doing working at one?"

"Trying to make enough money to pay next month's rent, if that's all right with you."

An odd choice of a job for a city woman, he thought. If she *was* a city woman.

She didn't have soft hands with prettily polished nails. Her fingers were long and strong-looking, her nails short. And she certainly wasn't model thin, all skin and bones, like a lot of the young women he'd seen since arriving in Chicago the day before. Thankfully. He always had admired a female with some curves on her.

But he was here to find a calf, Neil reminded himself again, not a woman.

"Actually," she went on, "I like this job a lot better than most of the ones I've had the past few years—''

Neil couldn't stop himself from interrupting. ''What kinds of jobs?''

''Waitressing, clerking in a department store, managing a coffeehouse, word processing for a law office—that was the worst—substitute teaching, telemarketing…well, the list goes on, but at least here, with the animals, I can almost pretend that…'' She suddenly seemed to catch herself and shook her head. ''Never mind.''

Neil wanted to ask Annabeth what she'd meant to say, wanted to ask why a sadness had passed through her expression. But he expected she wouldn't welcome either question. And to be truthful, he wasn't sure why he was interested.

Staring at the slight dimple in her chin, he said, ''Just tell me where my calf is and I won't take up any more of your limited time.''

''You have your draw?''

He showed her the slip of paper, clearly marked Casper, #9, Barn 1, Pen 3.

''Let's go see.''

But pen three in the far corner still stood empty.

Annabeth looked around as if she would find the calves wandering down the main aisle. ''Well, how in the world did I miss this?''

''You did say you were busy and shorthanded.'' Neil figured it wouldn't hurt to give her the benefit of the doubt.

''Right,'' Annabeth muttered. ''So why didn't you tell me a whole bunch of calves were missing?''

"I only want to find one—Casper."

"Casper, huh? Maybe he's a friendly ghost," she wisecracked. When he didn't return her unexpected smile, she said, "Ghost, as he's really here but you don't see him?" He merely raised his eyebrows and her grin faded. "Okay. Look, I don't know where he is right now, but when I get done—"

"Maybe you just misplaced him."

That stopped her cold. She gave him an intent look. "You mean, as in *me,* personally?"

"You don't seem overly enthusiastic about this job, so perhaps—"

"So perhaps what?" she asked, an indignant rise to her voice. "I'm automatically irresponsible?"

"I didn't say that."

"You didn't have to." Whipping around so fast that her ponytail nearly snicked him in the face, she started for the exit. "Come on."

"Where?"

"To find your calf."

Keeping his gaze pinned to that swinging ponytail rather than a certain part of her anatomy that was far too distracting, Neil started after her. "You think he's in one of the other barns?"

"All the calves are supposed to be in this one," she said, sailing through the open barn door. "But it won't hurt to check with Lloyd before sorting through these, looking at ear tags for the one with the number nine."

"Lloyd?" he echoed.

"Lloyd Wainwright, the stock contractor!"

That's right, she'd already mentioned him, Neil realized. He also recognized the fact that he was off his game. That Annabeth had distracted him from his purpose. And now he was practically jogging to keep up with her.

What in the world was wrong with him, giving her such a hard time when she was just trying to do her job?

Thinking he'd tell her to forget it, that she had enough on her plate to worry about, being short of help and all, he reached for her arm.

"Wait a minute."

The second his fingers came in contact with her flesh, his head seemed to explode...

Annabeth stands stock-still, big blue eyes wide and staring at something he can't see. Her breath comes in short spurts and she licks her lips once.

A trickle of sweat runs down the side of her forehead, trails her cheek and glistens along her jaw.

He can hear the beat of her heart...ba-bump...ba-bump...ba-bump...as palpable fear emanates from her in waves.

...Neil swayed and stumbled back.

"Hey, are you all right?" Annabeth stopped, her features softened by what looked like concern for him. "You're not sick or something, are you?"

"No, I'm fine. Just had a clumsy moment."

His heart thudded against the lie. He wasn't fine. Not by a long shot.

What the hell had just happened to him?

"You look like you really have seen a ghost," she said.

Or had some premonition.

The McKenna Legacy?

"I think I'm due for some food," Neil muttered. "But that can wait."

"No, really. You look all pale—"

"Let's go find Wainwright."

Annabeth gave him a doubtful expression but started off again, this time slower.

And Neil gave himself an internal shake. Just because he'd hit that magical thirty-third birthday didn't mean his grandmother's legacy had kicked in. He wasn't like his siblings or his McKenna cousins.

He was the pragmatic one.

Neil had always prided himself on being a straight shooter and hard worker with no illusions and, maybe regrettably, no sense of whimsy. He couldn't see through other peoples' dreams, wasn't empathic, didn't have an invisible connection with his animals.

So what the hell had just happened? he wondered again as he followed Annabeth through the crowd.

Though he'd been set to tell her to forget about Casper, now he couldn't, not until he'd figured it out. He'd seen Annabeth frightened. In danger. She'd been wearing the same yellow T-shirt and her hair had looked exactly the same, too, down to a yellow ribbon tying the ponytail. So if he really had experienced some kind of premonition, that probably meant danger wasn't far off.

"There he is," she said, pointing. "The big guy is Lloyd Wainwright."

A large, middle-aged man in an embroidered cowboy shirt and gray Stetson glanced over his shoulder as if looking for someone, while huddled in conversation with two others. An intricate squash-blossom necklace of silver and turquoise hung around the neck of one of them, an elderly Native American whose long steel-gray hair hung around his broad shoulders. The other man, a Hispanic, wore a fancy charro suit with engraved silver conchos. Neil guessed both of Wainwright's companions were connected with the rodeo somehow.

"What happened to them missing steers?" asked the Native American.

Drawing closer, Neil spotted his identification naming Peter Telek as the head of the rodeo committee.

"Can't really tell you, Pete," Wainwright said. "Flabbergasted me to hear we got some strays. I thought all the trucks came in, but maybe one broke down on the road and the message didn't get passed along like it should have been. I'll need some time to look into it."

Strays...Casper? Neil wondered.

The man in the charro suit muttered, "I hope there's no problem—no dead or hurt stock—or the animal rights activists will be after me."

Before Neil could figure out who the smaller man might be, Annabeth softly asked, "Lloyd, can I talk to you just for a minute?"

Wainwright turned toward them and gave them a big friendly smile. His pale gray eyes crinkled behind metal-framed glasses as he stepped closer.

"Annabeth, honey, what can I do for you?"

"More bad news for you, I guess, considering the conversation. We seem to be missing about a dozen calves, too," she said, just before all hell broke loose.

An explosion of sound behind them was topped by a booming voice. "Stop, thieves! Stop right where you are!"

Feet pounding the pavement warred with a distressed woman's wail.

Neil whirled around to see a middle-aged woman on the ground, a man trying to lift her, and three masked men waving handguns coming straight at them. Following a dozen yards behind were two uniformed Chicago police officers, both with guns drawn also.

"All of you!" The man who seemed to be the leader of the thieves swept the barrel of his revolver to cover Neil, Annabeth and the three men. "You're coming with us inside."

Wainwright demanded, "What's going on? Who in blazes do you think you are?"

"The man with the loaded gun." He put the tip of the barrel right up in the stockman's face, then took a nervous glance behind toward the policemen. "Don't give me a reason to use it and no one will get hurt. Now move!"

No one seemed inclined to argue. They moved.

"Don't do it!" one of the officers yelled. "Taking hostages is a lot more serious than armed robbery!"

But the thieves ignored him.

Neil's pulse thudded as the masked men swept them into the nearby press office without even hesitating. The room sat empty but for a single desk, several chairs and a telephone. The leader shucked off loaded saddlebags from his shoulder and deposited them on the desk.

As if he couldn't believe this was happening to him, the Hispanic asked, "Wainwright, are these men part of the rodeo entertainment?"

"Yeah, of course we are." The leader of the thieves answered and gave the Hispanic man a once-over. Then he waved a gun at the man's feet. "You, too, Pancho. Next thing you know, I'm gonna have you do a fancy dance for the crowd."

Dark eyes blazing, the man bristled as he seemed to grow an inch. "Do you know who you're speaking to?"

"Naw, go on and tell me."

"Alderman Salvador Lujan."

"A politician?" The thief snorted behind his mask. "I hate politicians. But thanks for the heads up. You may come in handy during the negotiations."

"What negotiations?"

"The cops are multiplying out there," said the thief closest to the windows.

"What do we do now?" the other asked, sounding panic-stricken. "How did we get into this mess?"

"Calm down. We need to keep our heads," the leader said.

This couldn't be a good thing, Neil thought—the criminals arguing among themselves. And the other men were getting restless, too, as if they had ideas about wrangling with the thieves whose attention was divided between them and the windows. He hoped no one was going to be so foolish as to try to be a hero. They could all be killed.

He glanced at Annabeth, not exempt from the consensus. She was trembling and staring at the masked leader as if she wanted to pummel him.

"Let's keep it together," he said in his most soothing voice.

Though he was really talking to her, he included the men by looking at them all.

Wainwright especially appeared steamed. Neil guessed he wasn't quiet by nature and it was taking some effort for him not to challenge the thieves. Before the stockman could lose his temper and blow up, Neil stepped in front of him, effectively placing himself square in the middle of a potentially explosive situation.

"Excuse me, but what is it that you want with us?" Neil asked the thief leader.

"Hell," the man said with another snort. "You're gonna be our hostages!"

Chapter Two

Hostages!

The very word struck fear into Annabeth's heart.

Already feeling that she was a hostage of this city that had stolen so much from her personally, she wasn't about to accept this situation lying down. Tough because life had forced her to be, she refused to give in to her fear and cower in some corner as if she was helpless. Instead, she decided to do what she could to help the police catch the thieves and bring them to justice later, after this was all over.

To that end, Annabeth surreptitiously eyed the three villains.

"More cops arriving," said the shortest of the thieves, his accent heavily Hispanic. He turned from the window, his eyes above the mask so dark a brown as to look black. "Won't be long before they call in the SWAT team. Then we're done for."

The barrel-chested Hispanic looked strong enough to bring down a steer in record time, Annabeth thought. He wore his shirtsleeves partially rolled up so that she spotted a tattoo on his left forearm. All

she could see was the bottom of the design—a red
rose.

"I can't go to jail again," complained the second
man, a slender African American whose café au lait
coloring and hazel eyes showed above his bandanna.
"I can't do more time. Uh-uh. Can't be locked up
again, not ever."

The nervous Nellie's free hand continually stroked
the barrel of the drawn revolver that was, at the moment, pointed toward the floor. If he wasn't careful,
Annabeth thought, he would shoot himself in the foot.
She gave his spanking-new boots a once-over—the
way he was rocking on the sides of his feet, they were
hurting him because they weren't broken in. And possibly because they weren't a proper fit.

Which made her think that he and his cohorts were
probably city boys playing dress up.

"You won't go to jail," the leader said, as again
he swept his revolver around the room at his hostages.
"None of us will, not as long as we have *them.*" His
skin was fair, almost pasty, and his pale gray eyes
held a glint of sheer meanness. Obviously agitated
despite his seeming confidence, he went to look out
the window himself, muttering, "Keep them covered."

Annabeth estimated him to be six feet tall—about
the same height as Neil Farrell—and figured the thief
worked out a lot to get that musculature in his arms
that showed through the sleeves of his shirt. Neil undoubtedly got *his* whipcord-hard build from years of
tough ranch work, she thought, glancing from one
man to the other and making comparisons. They

seemed nearly evenly matched, the thief having the slight edge of showy muscle over the rancher.

Yet she suspected Neil was as strong as they came.

"If we don't do something, they're going to kill us," Telek suddenly whispered.

"They wouldn't dare kill an alderman!" Lujan returned in an equally low voice. "That would be suicide. The mayor would have every policeman in the city after them, with instructions to shoot to kill."

An exaggeration, Annabeth thought, no doubt prompted by the man's inclination to self-importance.

Lloyd wiped flop-sweat from his face with his bare hand and moaned, "Oh, Lord, how did this happen? I can see it coming. We're all gonna die."

"Not if we don't do anything to upset them," Neil said, his manner reasonable, his stance oddly relaxed.

She wouldn't count Neil out, Annabeth decided, considering his calm, quiet air of authority. He might be afraid or angry on the inside, but he wasn't wearing either emotion where anyone could see it and use it against him.

"It wouldn't be in their best interests to add five murders to whatever else they've done," Neil added.

His gaze strayed over to the desk where the dumped saddlebags still sat.

Annabeth contemplated the contents of the leather pouches—money, obviously.

Armed robbery, one of the policemen had shouted.

From the criminals' appearance—the new cowboy duds—they no doubt had dressed up to be inconspicuous when they hit the rodeo bank. But then the robbery had somehow gone bad, turning the tables on them.

And on the five people who just happened to be in their getaway path, a thought that rankled Annabeth.

When would the bad luck stop? she wondered.

She was tired of the fates dealing her a rotten hand every time she turned around.

Enough was enough!

"Don't let your fears get to you," Neil went on with sufficient confidence that he earned the attention of the other hostages. "Just keep calm, and everything—"

The lead thief suddenly tore away from the window, saying, "All of you, listen to this guy. He's talking sense. You don't give me no trouble and I let you walk outta here with us, skin intact, and then let you go when we get free of the cops. Is that a deal, or what?"

"Yeah, sure, sounds good to me," Peter Telek said.

"I'm for it," Lloyd mumbled.

Alderman Lujan muttered, "You better let us go or it's on your heads."

"What did you say?" the leader asked, drawing closer. "Was that a threat?"

"No!" Neil quickly placed himself between the thief and Lujan. He glanced over at the big-mouthed politician and gave him a look that kept him silent. "No threats here. We all want the same thing. To get out of this alive."

To all appearances, Annabeth thought Neil was in control of the room, at least of the other hostages, who were all looking to him for leadership now, as if he was their protector. And Neil didn't even have a weapon.

She inspected him more closely, noticing for the first time that the face below the brimmed tan hat was ruggedly attractive. His mouth was wide, his lower lip full. Sexy. And his eyes were an unusual shade of pale brown. Amber with yellow flecks, reminding her of a wolf's eyes.

The thought slid along Annabeth's spine, made her shudder slightly, as she considered the raw power of his personality, until now hidden by his calm demeanor.

And as if he could feel her reaction to him, Neil Farrell turned his head slightly and locked gazes with her.

For a moment he held her fast, unable to blink, unable to breathe, unable to think.

Her body wasn't frozen of feeling, however. She felt seared from her toes to her scalp, not to mention all the delicious places in between. The connection seared her nerves, too, and made her itchy to move.

To do *something*.

Annabeth forced her lashes down so she didn't have to look at Neil anymore. With effort, she even sucked in some air. The release from tension wasn't immediate, but she felt her control return.

What the heck was she thinking, getting all weak-kneed and goo-goo-eyed over a man, when she needed to be stronger than ever?

The fates weren't going to get her this time! she

vowed, again surreptitiously focused on the men holding them hostage.

"So, what are we gonna do?" asked the one with the tattoo. "How are we gonna make a break for it?"

Before the leader could answer, the telephone shrilled, sending Annabeth up on her toes. She wasn't the only one startled, she noted. Every man in the room seemed just as shaken by the unexpected ringing.

"Aren't you going to answer that?" she asked, heart tripping a beat.

"What makes you think it's for me?"

"How do you know? Maybe someone out there wants to make you an offer you can't refuse."

"She might be right," agreed the Hispanic thief, who was staring out the windows. "A truck just pulled up out there."

"They give us a way out, you take it," said the other man, still fondling his gun as the phone continued to ring. "No way am I gonna sit in no jail cell, even if I gotta shoot my way outta here."

"No one shoots anyone or anything until I say so!" the leader snapped. He looked at Annabeth and indicated the telephone. "You answer it."

Annabeth looked to Neil. He nodded.

She approached the desk, making certain she did nothing he could interpret as suspicious. Willing her hand to remain steady, she picked up the receiver and put it to her ear.

"Hello?" she whispered.

Suddenly her throat didn't want to cooperate. It felt dry and raw as if scraped by something harsh. And her heart, it felt as if it were trying to pound its way out of her chest.

"This is Sergeant Michael Hartmann," came a man's voice, deep with authority. "I'm with the police negotiations unit. Is everyone in there all right?"

"Yes, so far."

"Good. Let's keep it that way. Let me talk to one of them—whoever seems to be in charge."

"All right." Pulse racing madly, Annabeth held out the receiver to the leader. "It's for you, after all."

His gray eyes narrowed on the phone in her hand for a few long seconds. For a moment she thought he might refuse it, then he snatched it from her and put it to his face so that the receiver sat under the bandanna disguising him.

"Yeah?" he barked, then listened for a minute. "What? You think I'm stupid? You don't get my name, *Michael*. We ain't buddies." Another pause. "That's easy. We just want out of here. Safe passage."

Annabeth nearly dropped with relief. He was going to be reasonable and they were going to be rescued.

Or so it seemed for a moment...

"Now why would I want to let one of them go?" the leader asked. "We do that a few times and then you have no reason not to shoot."

She froze. This wasn't going smoothly, after all.

"Good faith, bull! Take it or leave it!" he barked, checking his watch. "You have fifteen minutes to decide. If I don't hear from you, I can't guarantee the hostages' safety." He looked directly at Annabeth when he said, "Oh, yeah—the woman will be the first to die."

Something in Annabeth died right there.

Die. Of course.

The leader slammed the receiver back into the cradle and stormed the wall with the windows so that he could peer out.

"They gonna do it?" asked the Hispanic.

"They have to," the third man said. "They don't want no one dead."

"We'll see."

We'll see?

So this was to be her fate...

Everything else had been taken away from her, so Annabeth didn't know why she was surprised. She was shaking inside and trying not to show it. Her stomach twisted, threatening her with the little food she'd had for breakfast. Yeah, right, that's all she would need, she thought, taking a deep breath to steady herself. Throwing up would impress the heck out of the three villains...

Neil must have sensed her private panic, for he caught her eye and motioned to her to come closer where he was leaning on the edge of the desk.

Her response was automatic. She did as he indicated and used the desk edge to steady herself.

If she thought Neil was going to give her a pep talk, she was wrong. All he did was catch her hand and hold it. Warmth surged through her and she sensed his strength of purpose. Her world began to right itself, despite the fact that the other hostages couldn't seem to look her way.

"How can you remain so calm through all this?" she asked softly.

"What good would anything else do?"

"Are you always so reasonable?"

"Except when I'm looking for a lost calf."

He was trying to make her smile, Annabeth realized. Too bad her sense of humor had fled with the comment about her being the first to die.

Still, neither of them mentioned that.

"So what is it you like about this particular job?" Neil asked her.

"The animals," she said before she could even wonder why he was questioning her about something so far removed from their imminent situation. "Working with them reminds me of a past life."

"You're old enough to have a past?"

His idea of a joke, she guessed. She forced a smile. "Okay, I meant when I was young."

"You're not exactly ancient now."

"Sometimes I feel ancient."

Like at the moment. Like when she was ten minutes away from death...no, more like seven now, she realized. At least three minutes must have passed.

"Why?" he asked, his apparent interest keeping at least part of her mind focused on something other than the threat. "Feeling ancient, I mean."

"Too many bad things," Annabeth said, remembering. "I was just eighteen when my parents lost the farm that had been in our family for four generations. They just couldn't make it anymore. So we packed up and moved to the big city to survive. Instead of going to college as planned, I went to work."

"That was a long time ago."

"It seems like yesterday."

Ten years gone. Wasted.

What had she accomplished with the life that would soon be snuffed out by some greedy bastard who chose not to make an honest living like most of the population?

"What are you two up to?"

Startled by the nearness of the vile voice, Annabeth jerked and faced the gray eyes scowling down at her.

"Nothing," she choked out. *The woman will be the first to die* echoed in her head. "We're just talking, that's all."

He rounded the desk. "How do I know you're not planning an escape attempt?"

Neil said, "Because we're too smart to do anything but cooperate."

"If I find out differently—"

"Leave her alone!" Telek shouted.

That seemed to surprise the thief as much as it did her. He backed off and switched his attention to the old Indian whose dark eyes spat contempt at the masked man.

"What's the matter, Chief?" he asked, voice silky. And deadly. "Am I on to something?"

"The girl didn't do anything to you," Lloyd mumbled. "That's all he's saying."

"Then maybe I *should* leave her alone. Maybe one of you wants to die."

He was playing with them, now pretend-shooting each of the three men, pointing his barrel from one to the other, using sound effects to mimic the shots.

"No, don't kill me!" Alderman Lujan protested. "You can't kill a family man. What would my wife and children do without me? Who would support them?"

"Your kids are in college," Telek groused. "And your wife has a good job with the city."

"I still am the main support of the family!" Lujan turned to the thief leader. "You were right in the first place to threaten the woman. No one likes to see a woman hurt. Go ahead and use her! The authorities will respond to that."

"Keep your mouth shut," Neil said with a steely resolve. "Or I'll shut it for you."

"You dare threaten me? I have power in this city. I can make it difficult—"

"Oh, shut up!" The leader raised his revolver. "I'm sick of your whining and threats."

Then too fast for anyone to anticipate him, he smacked the gun across the alderman's head so hard that blood dribbled down his face. And then the big-mouthed, small-spirited man slumped to the ground unconscious.

"Now, anyone else have anything to say?"

Repulsed by the violence, Annabeth felt her heart thud against her ribs. Her pulse raced so fast she feared it would tear through her arteries. She'd seen violence like this before. This was only the start. Someone would be in bloody bits before this situation was brought to an end.

Starting with her!

The woman will be the first to die.

She believed it now—if Lujan wasn't already dead,

that was. On the floor next to him, Telek checked for vital signs. His fingers pressed against the alderman's throat, he grunted and nodded.

Annabeth drew a shaky breath.

She had to get out of there, somehow, before her life spun totally out of control. It *was* out of control, she thought. What she had to do was to reel it back in.

She had to do *something* to save herself.

"I won't let anything happen to you," Neil said softly, as if he'd read her mind.

Too late for assurances—the violence had already begun. She wanted to believe him, only she couldn't.

Save herself.

She had to.

But how?

Her blood felt thick, her limbs heavy, her head light.

She scanned the room. Only one way out—the door guarded by the nervous Nellie, who was pacing before it. Distracted. The Hispanic was staring out the window at the gathering authorities. And in a few minutes their leader would be occupied on the telephone.

It would have to be then, she thought, plotting at triple speed. Surely every man in the room would be focused on that conversation, all but the one on the phone, only guessing what the negotiator might be saying from the other end.

The woman will be the first to die.

As if he heard the refrain echoing in her head, Neil touched her arm. The breath hissed through his teeth and he froze, staring at her, his wolf eyes so intense she shuddered.

He was acting as he had when he'd touched her in front of the barn.

The shrill of the phone made Neil let go.

Annabeth's heart began to pump again as she moved away from him on legs of wood. "Should I answer that?"

"Nah, I'll get it," the thief said, closing in on the phone as she moved away from it.

Annabeth could feel Neil's eyes, could almost hear him begging her not to go through with her plan.

"You had your ten minutes, so what's your answer?" she heard the thief ask.

A feeling of unreality filling her, Annabeth backed toward the door. As she'd suspected, all eyes were glued to the man on the phone.

All eyes but Neil's.

The wolf eyes followed *her.*

"Wrong answer," the leader was saying. "Too bad for the woman…"

Annabeth moved as fast as she could and yet had the unreal feeling of moving in slow motion. But now was the moment. Purposely, she tromped the nervous thief's sore feet, and when he squawked in pain and did an awkward dance, she lunged for the door.

Her hand grasped the knob…the door opened…one foot slipped outside.

Then her head jerked back…followed by her body…her hair caught in a vise.

The leader had her by the ponytail. He plunged a

hand to the door, threatening her only chance at freedom.

At life!

Seeing red, she screamed and struck out hard to free herself, her fingers tangling in something soft as she tried to pull away. But he didn't let go.

She jerked her hand free and whipped her head around to see how she could fight him and realized what she had done.

The mask—she'd somehow managed to pull it down and she saw every detail of his face!

Annabeth averted her eyes as if she hadn't seen anything.

The villain jerked her around. The mask was back in place. And a gun barrel was inches from her forehead. She stared into the little round, dark circle that spelled her death.

"Nickels, don't be stupid!" hissed the Hispanic so softly that she might have imagined it.

But she wasn't imagining the danger she'd dared by trying this escape. Fear crept through her and squeezed her heart so hard that she thought it might burst from her chest.

The woman will be the first to die...

Chapter Three

Annabeth stood stock-still, her big blue eyes wide and staring at the gun pointed at her.

Muscles bunched, Neil slipped off the desk silently, his focus on the woman.

Her breath was labored and she licked her lips.

Just like in his premonition.

He could see the trickle of sweat that ran down the side of her forehead, trailed her cheek and glistened along her jaw. And he swore he could hear her heartbeat against the silence of the small room.

…ba-bump…ba-bump…ba-bump…

Fear oozed from her in waves as thieves and hostages alike stood transfixed, no one making a move, no one making a sound. Until…

The sharp *snick* of the hammer being drawn back on the revolver decided him.

Neil lunged for the thief before he could pull the trigger and blow Annabeth's brains out. Wrapping an arm around the would-be murderer's neck, Neil wrestled him down to the ground as he would a steer. Then, grabbing on to the man's gun hand, Neil slammed it to the floor.

The revolver skittered off.

With a huge twist, the thief used his greater weight to shift Neil from his back. A closed fist then connected with his jaw, sending him flying.

"Neil!" Annabeth cried. "Watch out!"

The room spun, but still Neil saw the thief go after his jettisoned revolver.

Other guns turned toward him so he rallied fast and flung himself forward and knocked the bigger man to the side.

They tussled, threw mostly ineffective punches and rolled across the floor. The thief struck out. Another fist smacked into the side of Neil's face. His head snapped back, and before he could recover, he felt fingers closing around this throat. He tried to break the hold, but the thief threw his greater weight to the side and rolled them both, with the man landing on top and losing his hat in the process.

Neil gasped at the combination of weight straddling his chest and pressure paralyzing his throat.

"Stop!" Annabeth yelled. "You'll kill him!"

"That's the idea!"

"Do it quick, then," one of his men said. "Those are reinforcements arriving."

Even as the other added, "Damn, it's the SWAT team! We're never gonna get outta here alive," a blur of yellow came hurtling toward Neil.

Annabeth crashed into the thief's side, breaking his stranglehold. Neil sucked in much-needed air and tried to clear his head even as, while still straddling him, the thief grabbed for Annabeth's arm.

The moment the connection was complete, inexplicable power suddenly shot Neil into a whirling vortex…

Annabeth hurries, looking over her shoulder.

Behind her, a city neighborhood, dark and deserted, eerily lit.

A rapid-transit train overhead breaks the silence…clack-clack…clack-clack…clack-clack…

Throwing another look over her shoulder, she gasps.

And the pulse of the train softens into a rapid heartbeat…clack-clack…ba-bump…clack-clack…ba-bump…ba-bump…

Neil can't see more than a man's silhouette, but he recognizes the danger…

The thief exploding into movement shattered the trance and Neil started, blinking to clear his head as the bigger man let go of Annabeth, grabbed his hat and jammed it onto his head as he shot to his feet.

"Come on!" the leader roared. "Let's get out of here right now!"

He went for his gun, but to Neil's surprise, Annabeth was quicker, snatching it up and aiming with both hands. She held it on him as if she knew how to use it.

The leader glanced at the saddlebags on the desk, but he would have to get past Neil and an armed Annabeth to get them. He seemed to change his mind about wanting them and put a hand on the doorknob.

"Let's be quick about getting out of here," he told his men.

"What about the money?" the Hispanic asked.

The other insisted, "I can't do no jail time! We gotta take hostages."

The leader glanced from Annabeth, who was crouched against the wall and appeared ready to shoot if he approached her, to the alderman, who was getting to his feet.

"Forget the money and we need just one hostage," the thief muttered. "I knew you would come in handy, Chico." He indicated the alderman. "Get him!"

Perhaps it was because Lujan cried, *"No, not me. I'm a family man! The woman, remember, get the woman!"* that the others hesitated to jump to his aid when the men grabbed him and dragged him to the door.

"Where do we—"

"Follow the plan!"

It all happened so fast that Neil had no time to move before they were out the door. Not that he could have stopped them with two of them still armed in any case. He wasn't stupid enough to chance a bullet.

A *clunk* made him turn to see Annabeth, hands empty. She had dropped the gun at her feet and she was shaking.

No, he wouldn't be that stupid, unless it was to save some woman desperate enough to make a break for it when she should have stayed put, Neil amended.

Shots rang out and he hit the wall next to the window where he could see out. The nervous thief, trigger-happy and shooting at anything that moved, was cut down in seconds. He sprawled across the pavement, leaving trails of blood spiderwebbing out from his body.

But the other two, still with Lujan as a shield, cut

right into the gathering crowd and disappeared from view.

"Damn! They got away," Neil said, even as armed, uniformed men were deployed after them. He turned to the others. "It's over, at least for us. Just hope they don't hurt Lujan."

Wainwright removed his hat and wiped at his sweaty face with a handkerchief. "I thought we were dead men."

Telek nodded at Neil. "We might have been if not for you."

"Right, and you saved my life for sure," Annabeth said. Her arms were wrapped around her middle as if to stop the shaking. "How can I ever thank you?"

"By not ever pulling a stunt like that again," he gritted out.

Her expression closed. "I—I'm sorry. I thought he really would shoot me to make a point. I panicked...I—I wasn't thinking..."

Her obvious contrition softened Neil. "What's done is done. No use worrying about it now."

Her panic was understandable, considering the thief had threatened her directly.

And the threat wasn't over.

Just as had happened earlier, he'd seen what the future held. Annabeth had been the focus of both visions.

Somehow the thief had made the connection between him and Annabeth when he'd grabbed her arm. Or maybe they were all three connected, the thief himself being the danger.

Annabeth *had* seen his face, after all. He'd seen the mask come down, but she'd been in the way and he hadn't seen the guy's face himself. She was the only one who could make a positive identification. No surprise if the bastard came after her to keep her from fingering him.

Neil knew she was in danger, but how could he convince anyone else, even her? How could he tell anyone what he knew, when he was having trouble taking it all in himself? He'd never before this day experienced a precognitive moment, so he didn't have a clue as to how to handle it.

If he warned the police, what would he say? That he'd *seen* Annabeth in danger earlier, and then what he'd seen in his vision had really happened. Would they believe it?

No way, he decided. They would think he was a kook. And that meant they wouldn't take his seeing her in danger a second time seriously. So there was no point in telling them something they wouldn't want to hear.

The door crashed open and uniformed members of the SWAT team, guns at the ready, penetrated the room.

If they had come sooner, like *before* Annabeth had seen the thief's face, he might not be so weighted down by the responsibility of making sure she was safe.

"Nice to see you guys, even if you are a little too late," Neil said dryly.

Whether or not he liked it, until the thieves were caught, Annabeth Caldwell was his concern.

"THE HOSTAGE AND Barricaded Suspect Team was getting into place just as the criminals made their move," Detective Dan Wexler explained. "We were in the process of deploying the snipers when they ran."

Annabeth figured Detective Wexler to be in his early forties despite the silver feathering thick brown hair that framed a craggy face and vivid blue eyes that crinkled around the corners. He was tall and trim and neatly pressed. His air of authority was comforting rather than intimidating.

"The man who was shot," she asked, suddenly having trouble breathing, "is he dead?"

"Yes, ma'am. The other two got clean away. Our men are working the crowd. But under the circumstances..." He shrugged.

Despite the fact that crime-scene tape limned the perimeter, Annabeth felt the crowd closing in on her. People of all ages were hanging around, trying to pick up some tidbit about the robbery and hostage situation. While his partner was interviewing Lloyd Wainwright and Peter Telek inside the office, Wexler had taken her and Neil to a bench outside to hear their account of the story.

"Did they wear gloves at all times?" Wexler asked, leg lifted, polished shoe resting on the edge of their bench.

Neil shook his head. "Never took them off that I noticed."

"Too bad. No fingerprints to lift. I thought maybe we would find some on the saddlebags."

"Maybe you still can," Neil suggested. "Who's to say these guys were smart enough to wipe it clean of their prints before they set off for the robbery?"

"Good point. The evidence techs will be thorough. If there's a fingerprint to be gotten, they'll find it."

"At least they didn't get away with the money," Annabeth said, "not that it's as important as a lost life. Even a criminal's life. Hopefully not Lujan's life."

"If they're smart," Wexler said, "they'll keep Lujan safe. As for the thief—he wouldn't have been shot if it hadn't been absolutely necessary."

"I saw it all," Neil told her. "That guy was going crazy shooting off his revolver. Probably emptied it. He could have killed someone else. He had to have known what would happen to him when he didn't just try to get away clean. I guess he was afraid of being caught and serious about never going back to jail."

She nodded. "He asked for it, then."

Like her brother had asked for it. But Larry had been a good little boy and a great kid. Unfortunately, he'd grown into a teenager confused by those who pretended to be his friends.

And this city was so unbearably unforgiving of mistakes.

Shoving the memory away, she said, "I can give you a description of one of the men. That would help you catch him, right?"

"I thought the men were masked at all times."

"They were. Except I got a look at the leader—the one the other guy called Nickels."

"Nichols?" Wexler repeated, making a notation in his little black book. "I'll run it through our criminal database to see if we can get a handle on a perp who fits your description." He gazed at her intently. "So, you got a look at the leader of the gang without his mask.''

"Just for a minute."

Annabeth shuddered. She had come so close to dying that she struggled with the memory. Swallowing hard, she stared down at her hands in her lap, all twisted together as she fought her nerves. Neil reached over and just for a second covered her fidgeting fingers and gave them a light squeeze of reassurance. Unexpected warmth filled her and eased her anxiety enough so that she was able to go on.

"I'll never forget his face," she whispered, picturing it now. "Narrow. Steely-gray eyes and thin lips. A tight mouth. And a faint, white scar here." She touched the soft area under her right cheekbone.

"Good." Wexler was writing furiously in his notebook. "That will help. I'll bring you down to the area office and you can work with Officer Nuhn. We use a computer program now to fit the pieces together and come up with a likeness."

"I can come along, as well," Neil said. "I had direct contact with the man." He smoothed a hand over his aching jaw. "I may think of something, be able to help in some way."

Wexler nodded. "Good, good."

"But you have a timed event that you're supposed to compete in," Annabeth protested.

"Today it was just for show. I don't need the practice. Besides, no Casper, remember?"

Reminded of the missing calves, she wondered what could have happened to them.

Missing calves...missing steers...missing thieves...

Wexler had a few more questions, but he wound

up the interview within minutes. "I'll just tell my
partner I'm taking you two to the station."

"I need to talk to my boss for a minute, as well,"
Annabeth said. "He'll have to get someone to cover
for me."

Neil nodded. "I'll wait out here."

She quickly followed the detective back into the
building.

Lloyd seemed uncommonly quiet for a normally
talkative man. Peter Telek was engaged in a dialogue
with Detective Ben Smith, a wiry African American
in jeans, running shoes and a Bulls T-shirt, as different from Wexler as he could be. Lloyd seemed to
have closed himself off from the interview. He leaned
back slightly in his chair, his arms crossed over his
chest like a barrier to more questioning. Annabeth
wondered where that interview had gone sour.

When Wexler interrupted Smith, Annabeth approached her boss.

"Lloyd, Detective Wexler asked me to go to the
station with him—"

"What for?"

"Because I saw the leader's face. He wants me to
help them get a computer image of the guy."

He blinked at her through his metal-rimmed
glasses. "But I need you here."

"Are you saying I can't get off work?"

A moment of silence stretched between them before Lloyd shrugged his shoulders and said, "Of
course, of course. You have to do whatever you can
to make sure that villain is caught," he said, forcing
a familiar smile. "Don't worry your pretty little head,
I'll get someone to take care of the calves. And don't

worry about coming back here today. You go home and rest those nerves of yours.''

"Home, right," she said without enthusiasm. "Thanks, Lloyd. I'll make it up to you, I promise."

"I'm sure you will, Annabeth, honey, I'm sure you will."

"You might want to be careful how involved you get in this case," Peter Telek said.

Annabeth started at the warning. Turning to him, she met a face of stone. "Why?"

"Because it's bound to turn out bad for you."

A thrill shot up her spine, and gooseflesh spread along her limbs. "Bad...how?"

"He'll find you," the old man predicted. "They always do."

Annabeth backed away from him. Great. Just what she needed—dire predictions from someone she didn't even know. Nickels stalking her...

She couldn't get back outside fast enough.

Neil was waiting for her. Focusing on him made her feel a bit better, a bit less on edge. He was a man with a solid feel, one a woman could count on, she thought.

But focusing on him brought to her attention something that she had missed. Or perhaps overlooked in light of her own emotional upheaval.

"Your face—it's bruised. And your neck. Nickels really hurt you!" She stepped closer and raised a hand as if to touch his face, then changed her mind when she realized she might make him hurt more. "Maybe you should see someone. Get checked over."

"I'm fine."

She swallowed hard. "You don't look fine, especially your neck."

"I'm just bruised is all," Neil insisted as Detective Wexler left the office.

"Ready to go?"

They followed him to the street, where his vehicle waited. But before they could get in, a squad car pulled up to the curb and the driver's door opened.

"Wexler," the officer who slid out said, "we've retrieved our hostage."

"What about the thieves?"

"Never saw them. We found Alderman Lujan wandering through the crowd, kind of, uh…talking to himself. Apparently, the thieves just let him go."

He opened the rear door and the alderman stumbled out, looking a bit dazed. The moment he saw Annabeth, however, he pointed a shaky finger at her.

"You! This is all *your* fault. You put me in danger. I heard what you did. I wouldn't have been taken hostage, my life threatened, if you hadn't stirred things up with that fool escape attempt."

"I'm sorry," Annabeth said, her spirits plummeting once more.

"Sorry isn't good enough—"

"Whoa!" Neil stepped forward so that he was shielding her from the angry politician. "The lady apologized. She thought her life was in immediate danger. You can't hold that against her."

"I certainly can!"

Detective Wexler stepped in. "Alderman Lujan, we need your statement. My partner is just finishing up with the other hostages. He'll take care of you.

Officer, would you escort the alderman inside. And if he needs anything, see that he gets it.''

Lujan narrowed his gaze at Annabeth and shook a finger at her. ''I'm not through with you, yet,'' he warned before stalking off with the officer in tow.

''Don't worry about the alderman,'' Wexler said. ''He tends to overdramatize. He's upset, but he'll cool down.''

Upset? Annabeth thought. He wasn't the only one.

As if he could read her thoughts, Neil put an arm across her back and lightly rubbed her arm. Annabeth suppressed a gasp in reaction.

''C'mon. Forget that loudmouth. You have more important things to take care of.''

''Uh-huh.''

Right now she was thinking about him. About his hand touching her, stroking her. She fought the insanity and let him help her into the back seat of Wexler's car. He then slid in next to her.

On their way to the area office, Neil reinforced that notion of solidity that she had about him. As they sped through the Loop area, he distracted her and kept her talking about her various jobs until the last of her nerves dissipated.

''So, that lawyer you worked for…you say he was condescending?''

''And an idiot in general,'' she added with a weak grin.

''How did he get on your bad side?''

''The morning I showed up on the job, he said he had a backlog of letters for me to type and handed me an audiotape, then left,'' Annabeth remembered. ''I got myself set up with the computer and Dictaphone, but when I played back the tape, his voice kept going in and out. It was weird—he must have stopped and started a hundred times. I suspect he didn't really know how to use the machine.''

"But you told him," Neil said with a smirk.

"Well, I tried to be tactful. Really." But she couldn't help grinning at the memory. "When I told him about the problem, he grabbed the tape from my hand, said *it* was obviously defective and chucked it in the wastebasket.''

Neil chuckled. "Ooh, a little defensive. What then?"

"Then he told me to do some task I didn't exactly understand. And when I asked for an explanation, he said he didn't give instructions, turned his back on me and walked out of the office. I waited for nearly an hour, but he never came back. And there was no one else to ask. Finally, I just got disgusted enough to leave.''

"And that ended your word processing career?"

She nodded. "Of course, he told the agency that *I* was incompetent.''

They laughed together and Annabeth felt better than she had all day. No, even longer. Maybe all year.

Glad that she didn't have to go through this ordeal alone, no matter the reason they were getting along so well after a bad start, she clung to the lifeline of connection with another human being that Neil held out to her, if even for a short while. Bad enough that she would be alone later.

Even with support, however, she hated having to enter another police station. The wounds were still too raw. But remembering Telek's warning, she knew she had to shelve her personal prejudice to help catch a *real* criminal.

Detective Wexler introduced them to Officer Laura Nuhn and then disappeared. The policewoman was a young, pretty brunette with a quiet demeanor.

"This way," she said, leading Annabeth and Neil into her cubicle. "Make yourselves comfortable."

Annabeth sat next to the policewoman, and Neil stood behind them as Nuhn set up her program.

Too aware of Neil's presence, Annabeth began to squirm inside. When he leaned over for a better look at the monitor, his hip brushed her shoulder and she shifted in her seat. His tendency to do natural things, like placing his hand on the back of her chair, distracted her.

And so it took some effort to focus when Officer Nuhn finally said, "Let's begin with the shape of the face."

She called up a screen of different face shapes.

Annabeth tapped at the one that reminded her of Nickels. "Long and narrow."

Nuhn seemed so expert with her computer that Annabeth wondered if the policewoman had been born using one. Her long fingers continually flew over the keyboard as she asked questions.

"What about his hair? Color, texture, hairline, style?"

"He was wearing a brimmed hat," Annabeth said. "It came off for a moment, but that's when his back was to me. All I can tell you is that it was medium brown and a little shaggy around the neckline."

"I got a close-up of the hair since he was on top

of me,'' Neil said wryly. ''Thick but with a widow's peak.''

The long and narrow face on the monitor suddenly sprouted a hairline.

''What about his forehead?'' Nuhn asked. ''High or low?''

''High.''

The forehead stretched a bit.

''Smooth, creased or wrinkled?''

''Smooth,'' Neil continued.

''Tell me about his eyes. Color, shape, what kind of eyebrows?''

Annabeth said, ''Pale gray and narrow. His eyebrows were kind of flat.''

They went through dozens of details, including the shape of his nose and nostrils, the size and prominence of his ears, the line of his mouth, the shape of the chin and the condition of his complexion.

The face on the monitor was starting to look eerily familiar.

''Don't forget the scar,'' Annabeth said, ''under his right cheekbone.''

The policewoman added the final detail.

''There. What do you think?'' Officer Nuhn asked. ''Is that our thief?''

Annabeth considered it. ''His cheeks were a bit more angular.''

The policewoman fine-tuned the computer image. ''Anything else.''

''That's it,'' Annabeth whispered, thankful that she had been so observant.

Neil leaned past her to place a hand across the

lower half of the man's on-screen face as if it were a mask. "Yep. That's him, all right. You've got him."

If only that weren't merely a figurative statement, Annabeth thought as he brushed her once more. Her pulse picked up, but she told herself it was because she wanted Nickels caught and incarcerated before he could do more harm.

A moment later she held an actual printout of the thief's face in her hand.

"Kind of a macabre souvenir of our experience," she muttered as Detective Wexler rejoined them.

"That's Nichols?" he asked.

"A spitting image," she agreed.

"This woman is amazing," Neil said. "She didn't miss a thing."

"Good, since this is all we have for now. I ran the name through the database but we didn't find anyone who even came close to fitting your description. So we'll be relying on this composite to find him."

"How long do you think it might take?" Neil asked.

"I can't say. We could find him tomorrow."

Or never, Annabeth thought with a shiver. She carefully folded her copy of the printout and slipped it into a back pocket of her jeans.

"Since Annabeth is your chief witness," Neil went on, "you're planning on giving her round-the-clock protection, right?"

"Not really. She's in no danger."

"How do you know that?"

"The thieves don't even know her name, and we won't be releasing it to the media."

"But what if he finds out who I am?" Annabeth

asked. Now she not only had to dread being alone, she had to worry about it. "Nickels or his partner could ask around the festival grounds and find out where I work."

"Doubtful," Wexler said. "But just in case, perhaps you ought to take off for a few days."

"I can't afford to take off—I have rent to pay. Groceries to buy."

"Well, that's up to you. But if you should see Nickels or get wind of some stranger asking after you, get back to me and I'll see what I can do."

"So you can help *after* the fact," Neil said.

"Sorry. I might not like it any more than you do, but I can't argue with the system." Wexler's expression *was* apologetic. "Hang on a minute and I'll get you both a ride home."

Annabeth nodded. Now she was dreading the hours that would stretch out before her.

"What now?" Neil asked.

"What do you mean?"

"Are you really going to go home and rest like Wainwright told you to do?"

"I don't know. I hadn't thought about it. Why?"

"Well, I was just wondering…if you're up to it, I mean…would you mind spending a little more time with me?"

Despite the fact that he'd been her support system for the past few hours, Annabeth couldn't help giving him a suspicious expression. But his eyes were just eyes now, no trace of the wolf she had seen earlier. His rugged features actually looked kind of ordinary. And he was chewing on that full lower lip as he awaited her answer.

At the moment, Neil Farrell *seemed* pretty harmless.

"Define 'spend time.'"

"It's a family obligation. A birthday party. And I'll be the only one there without a date."

Date?

Annabeth shook her head. "I—I don't know—"

"You would really be doing me a big favor," Neil said. "Pretty please?"

"Well…"

As long as he put it that way, she was hard-pressed to refuse. Besides, the last thing in the world she wanted to do was to go back to an empty apartment so that she could dwell on her latest scare.

"All right," she finally said. "I guess spending a few more hours with you, pretending to be your date, wouldn't hurt anything."

Chapter Four

"Happy birthday to you. Happy birthday to you. Happy birthday, dear Ne-e-il, happy birthday to you..."

Annabeth stood at the back of the McKenna horde singing to the birthday boy. *Had to go to a birthday party. No date.* True and true. Neil had just left out one small detail—that this was *his* birthday celebration.

"Happy thirty-third!" cried the cousin who went by the odd name of Skelly.

For some reason the horde turned toward her, faces lit expectantly. Feeling color rise to her cheeks, Annabeth just wanted to go hide somewhere.

"All right, leave my friend alone," Neil groused, flashing a look loaded with guilt at Annabeth, "or you won't get any birthday cake."

Grumbling, the family members relaxed and surrounded Neil, who was staring down at thirty-three lit candles.

"Make a wish, boyo," came a lilted command from the mahogany-haired Keelin. "'Tis bound to come true on this of all birthdays."

"Superstition," Neil joked, his gaze locking with Annabeth's.

For a moment something odd passed through his wolf eyes, making Annabeth wonder if she was the only one in the room who'd noticed. A thrill shot through her down to her toes. Then Neil lowered his head and blew.

And blew...and blew...and blew until every single candle was out.

A roar of approval rent the air and the adults began talking all at once. Three generations of family, Annabeth thought enviously. Skelly and his wife, Roz, and their redheaded toddler triplets—Bridget, Brendan and Briana. Also Skelly's brother, Donovan, and his very pregnant wife, Laurel, his sister, Aileen, and their father, Raymond. And then cousin Keelin, her husband, Tyler, and their toddler, Kelly, and his teenage daughter, Cheryl. And finally there was Keelin's brother, Curran, and his new wife, Jane, who'd driven up from Kentucky for their honeymoon.

Keeping all the McKennas and spouses and offspring straight was making her head spin, Annabeth thought.

And making her feel somewhat like an intruder.

With all eyes on the cake being cut with vigor, if not precision, by a laughing Neil, she took the opportunity to slip out of the room and wander into the back patio where she lowered herself onto one of the padded lounge chairs.

Neil had said Skelly and Roz were looking for a bigger place now that the triplets were running around. The city town house was a little too confining for three rapidly growing children and all their toys. They wanted one of those old Victorians with lots of rooms and a big yard.

Annabeth admitted that sounded like a nice dream. But the town house was nice, too, as was the walled garden, lush with vegetation that reminded her of her *real* home. The rich scent of flowers permeated the air. Annabeth remembered her mother tending such a garden replete with climbing roses and a nook with a bench for reading or hiding or whiling away a few hours.

Sighing, Annabeth lay back and enjoyed the moment. A few feet away, tucked into a corner of the small city space, a fountain trickled. Mesmerized by the soothing sound of splashing water that blocked out city and people noise, she closed her eyes, just for a moment.

But the siren call of sleep whispered her name...

"Annabeth?"

She sat with a start to see a silhouette before her. She blinked and brought a woman bearing a cane into focus. "Oh, Jane, did I actually fall asleep?"

"You did seem to be in a different world." Jane offered her a piece of birthday cake. "Maybe the sugar in this will energize you, at least for a little while."

Annabeth swung her feet to the ground and took the cake. With a slight limp, Jane moved to the lounge chair opposite and, finding it with her hand first, carefully lowered herself, set the cane across the cushion behind her, then arranged her long skirts carefully around her legs.

Annabeth got that Jane was sensitive about her limp, but it was hardly noticeable, especially so because she had an elegance about her that drew attention away from anything negative. Her golden-streaked brown hair was crushed into soft curls at her neckline, which was just low enough to hint at a bit of cleavage.

In comparison, Jane Grantham McKenna made Annabeth feel ungainly and unfashionable, even though Neil had taken her home before coming here so that she could change out of her jeans and T-shirt and into a nice pair of cream trousers and a tangerine-colored silk blouse.

"So, you and Neil were held hostage together," Jane said. "Interesting."

About to take a bite of the birthday cake, Annabeth halted her fork in midair. "You sound amused."

"Not by the situation itself, just by the implications."

"What implications?"

"Neil hasn't told you about The McKenna Legacy?"

"No." She went ahead and took the bite of cake. "We really don't know each other."

"Don't worry, you will."

Annabeth nearly choked while swallowing. "We were merely thrown together by circumstances."

"*Dangerous* circumstances."

"Right."

"That's how it always starts," Jane said knowingly.

"How what starts?"

"Moira McKenna's legacy to her grandchildren. I'm sure Neil will get around to telling you about it." Before Annabeth could demand further explanation from her, Jane smoothly switched topics. "The McKennas can be an intimidating group when taken all at once. But individually we're pretty likable, at least most of the time. *We.* That sounds odd," she murmured dreamily. "Curran and I are a 'we' already."

"Of course, you're married."

"But we haven't known each other very long. Barely three months, actually."

Annabeth didn't comment, but she thought rushing something so important as a lifetime commitment was a little foolish. "Congratulations," she said instead, trying to be more open-minded about it. "I guess it must have been love at first sight."

Jane laughed. "Hardly. We were brought together by a crazed Thoroughbred. I was put out by Curran and he was challenged by me. Not smooth sailing at the start. But all that changed. We went through so much together in a matter of a few days that it probably totaled what other couples might experience emotionally given months."

Was Jane trying to tell her something? Annabeth wondered, not feeling comfortable enough to ask for an explanation. No matter the events, however, she couldn't fancy falling in love so quickly. No way could you really get to know a person in a few weeks.

"So what sights are you and Curran planning on seeing while you're in Chicago?"

"Sights aren't important," Jane said. "People are.

Family. We came to see Curran's sister and cousins." She hesitated a moment, then added, "And for me to see a specialist at Northwestern Hospital."

"Nothing serious, I hope."

"Something very serious." But Jane was smiling. "It seems that I'm an excellent candidate for cartilage regrowth. They'll take some of my healthy cartilage, grow it in petri dishes and then put the new growth back in my knee." She patted her left leg. "If all goes as the surgeon predicts, my knee will be as good as new before Curran's and my first anniversary."

"That *is* good news."

"Then we can start working on a family of our own."

A family of her own...

Annabeth's mood dimmed a bit, but she managed to say with all sincerity, "I'm sure everything will work out for you exactly as you hope."

"Things will work out for you, as well," Jane predicted. "If you open your heart to the possibilities. And to Neil."

Annabeth's pulse thudded strangely even as she protested, "Neil and I just met today."

"Yes," Jane said, grinning. "I know. And what a terrible, wonderful adventure you are about to embark on."

Annabeth gaped at that, but before she could demand an explanation this time, footsteps alerted them to a male presence.

"Sheena," came a lilting, seductive voice from the doorway uttering the endearment. "I've been looking everywhere for you."

"Well, now you've found me, Curran, love." Jane pushed herself up and took her cane. "The McKenna Legacy—ask Neil about it."

Annabeth merely nodded and smiled as Jane joined her husband, whose black hair and deep blue eyes were striking. He looked at Jane with such love, that longing welled in Annabeth.

Would a man ever look at her that way? she wondered.

Which made her think about Jane's parting shot.

The McKenna Legacy...

Forget it, Annabeth told herself, going back to her cake. She wouldn't be around Neil McKenna Farrell long enough to get his family history.

"I DON'T KNOW what to think," Neil said, having just told his cousin Skelly about the two precognitive incidents that he'd experienced.

They were having a brandy in the den, which supposedly was Skelly's office where he'd written his first two novels, despite the toys littering nearly every surface. It now happened to be Neil's room for the week. He'd decided to tell Skelly what was on his mind since, until today, they'd had in common the fact that they'd both been left out of the McKenna woo-woo loop. Now, after that morning's experience, Skelly held that honor alone.

"Nothing like that has ever happened to me before," Neil said, trying to understand why he'd suddenly tuned in to the McKenna Precognition Network. "Now I feel...I don't know...like I'm responsible for Annabeth."

"You're linked to her, all right, cuz," Skelly said, grinning. "Congratulations."

"What?"

Donovan entered the room, saying, "It is your time, after all—"

Skelly and Donovan were ganging up on him as brothers often did. Half-brothers, Neil amended, though the men looked alike—both tall with dark hair and similar features. Both grinning at him.

"My being thirty-three doesn't have anything to do with this!" Neil protested.

"—and Annabeth is undoubtedly part of Moira's legacy to you," Donovan finished, heading for the wall unit where the decanter of brandy sat. "Our grandmother always does have good taste, even from the great beyond."

Resentful that the brothers were ganging up on him, Neil muttered, "I've never heard of anything so ridiculous."

Though secretly he'd been entertaining like thoughts. *Disturbing thoughts.*

Despite his good sense, Neil was more drawn to Annabeth than he was willing to admit to his cousins. Or to himself, for that matter. Someday, he had hoped to meet a quiet, steady woman, someone with a nature similar to his own, and together, they would build a life and a family.

He simply wasn't looking for a spirited, independent Annabeth Caldwell!

"I still have thirty-two days left to meet her," he mumbled to himself, thinking that their grandmother's legacy gave them until the thirty-third day after their thirty-third birthday.

"That you do," Donovan said.

"Certainly," Skelly agreed.

But both of them were grinning ear to ear like idiots. "Morons!"

Skelly choked back a laugh to say, "Tell me, cuz, what was your first impression of Miss Annabeth?"

Remembering her struggle with the sack of feed, Neil said, "That she had a nice...uh...that she was attractive if outspoken."

"And when did you first have a vision?" Donovan asked, swirling the brandy in his glass.

Since he'd missed the introductory part of the conversation, Neil brought him up to speed. "I irritated her and she went stalking off and I tried to stop her."

"So you had the vision when you touched her?" Donovan said.

"Right."

"Mmm." Donovan took a swallow of the liquor. "And you don't think that's significant?"

"I feel like we're connected, yes."

"Then you *aren't* fighting it."

"There are different ways of being connected," Neil insisted. "Like by a thief on the loose. By danger. *That* kind of connection."

"I think he's in denial," Donovan said.

"No doubt about it." Skelly arched an eyebrow at Neil. "Read Moira's letter lately?"

Neil didn't have to read it again. He'd already read his copy of the letter that Moira McKenna had sent to each of her nine grandchildren so many times since his sister Kate had put herself in terrible danger, that he knew it by heart.

He could see the well-worn, cream vellum sheet in his mind's eye...

To my darling grandchildren,

I leave you my love and more. Within thirty-three days of your thirty-third birthday—enough time to know what you are about—you will have in your grasp a legacy of which your dreams are made. Dreams are not always tangible things, but more often are born in the heart. Act selflessly in another's behalf, and my legacy will be yours.

Your loving grandmother,
Moira McKenna

P.S. Use any other inheritance from me wisely and only for good, lest you destroy yourself or those you love.

The *act selflessly in another's behalf* part stood out in Neil's mind. He began to fidget. To mentally scramble for a way out. But how could he? It wasn't in his nature to leave someone vulnerable and in danger to her own devices.

Uh-oh.

Chances were, he was doomed....

"YOU HAVE A NICE FAMILY," Annabeth said as she hunkered down in the passenger seat of Neil's truck. "A really *big* family. And close."

She sounded so wistful that he asked, "And you don't?" as he pulled the vehicle away from the curb.

"Not for a while. There's just Mom and me now. And I was never close to cousins or aunts or uncles."

"Mothers are good," Neil said, thinking of his own.

Rose McKenna Farrell had always been the glue of the family, ever since he could remember. He also remembered what it had been like all those years that she'd been estranged from her brothers James and Raymond. Then his cousin Keelin had arrived from Ireland and had changed everything. But until the McKenna triplets were reunited a few years back, there had been an indescribable sadness about his mother that she had tried to hide.

Kind of like Annabeth was doing now.

"So are you and your mother okay?" he asked, quickly adding, "You just sound...well, like you're missing something." He hoped that was tactful enough that she wouldn't take offense.

"I'm missing *her*. It's just that Mom's not the same person she used to be. Me, neither, I guess. And then a few months ago, she moved back to Lincoln to live with her sister. She'd had it with this city."

Neil wondered what Annabeth *wasn't* saying. What had happened a few months before? Not that it was any of his business, considering they didn't even know each other.

So, as he turned onto a main street and headed for the Old Town neighborhood where Annabeth lived, he kept the conversation neutral.

"Is that where you're from? Lincoln, Illinois?"

"I grew up on a farm that was a twenty-minute drive from Lincoln," she said.

So he'd been right in thinking she wasn't a city girl. No wonder she'd wanted to work for the rodeo. The animals undoubtedly reminded her of her former life. Perhaps a better life than she had now.

"Actually, Lincoln is only a few hours' drive from Chicago," she was saying, "but when you don't have a car, it might as well be on the moon."

"If you were so close to your mother, why didn't you move with her? It's obvious that you miss her."

"Of course I do. But there's nothing for me in rural Illinois anymore."

Again the wistfulness came through loud and clear, Neil thought. "But there was once?"

"Before we lost the farm. It's just not right, all those small operations being sucked up by big corporation farms. That land was in our family for four generations. It would have gone five or even more..."

"You would have run it?"

"With my brother." She hesitated a moment, then added, "He's gone now, too."

"I'm sorry. I do understand. Ranching isn't a sure thing, either."

"But at least your family is keeping it together."

"We've been pretty lucky, though the whole family isn't working the ranch. My sister, Kate, and her husband, Chase, help out during the busy times, but they're responsible for a mustang refuge, and Kate is a successful vet, as well."

"Someone mentioned a brother."

"Yeah, I have a brother, but not so you would know it." Neil was hard-pressed to keep his resentment from his tone. "Quinlan goes wherever the wind blows. Half the time we don't even know his where-abouts.'' Which upset their mother, especially. ''Adventure rather than ranching is in his blood, I guess.''

''Which you resent.''

''I sure could use his support,'' Neil agreed, guessing that he hadn't done such a good job at hiding his resentment, after all. ''I keep telling myself that ranching isn't for everyone, that Quin has the right to choose a different life's path, but he doesn't seem capable of choosing anything, so why can't he stick around and lend a hand? It's getting harder to make a living every day.''

Which he knew personally, since his father had retired and turned over the reins to him. Of course, in a ranching family, being retired only meant that you didn't work twelve hours a day, seven days a week anymore. Except during calving and branding and roundup, that was.

But his father no longer did the books or the ranch budget or was in charge of paying off the loans. That all fell to Neil as ranch manager. The actual doing and the worrying that went along with the job.

''But we have such a wonderful economy.'' Annabeth sniffed. ''At least that's what the politicians keep telling us.''

Neil couldn't argue with that.

As a matter of fact, he hadn't argued with anything Annabeth had said all evening. And the evening was almost over. Already in the Old Town neighborhood, he pulled down the side street where she lived. Amazing, but they were getting along better than he'd expected.

Perhaps too well?

And then she said, "So tell me about The Mc-Kenna Legacy."

Which switched on all kinds of warning alarms for Neil. He pulled the truck into the only open spot on the overcrowded city street—next to a fire hydrant.

Feeling her staring at him, waiting for an answer, he caved. "How do you know about the legacy?"

"Jane mentioned it. She's a nice woman, but that conversation we had in the garden was a little on the strange side."

"I guess it would be to an outsider." Hell, it was even strange to him.

"She said something about a terrible, wonderful adventure that *I* was about to embark on."

"Mmm," he murmured, trying to sound noncommittal.

Which proved impossible when Annabeth added, "She made a big deal about you and me being thrown together under dangerous circumstances."

Sudden tension live-wired from her to him.

"Well, we were, this morning."

"She said that's how it always *starts*. How what starts? Jane said that I should ask you about it. What is this legacy all about?"

Oh, Lord, now he was going to have to tell her. Neil wondered how much he could edit out. He wasn't sure of anything and he didn't want to give her ideas that he himself found unsettling and unacceptable.

"Okay, let me start at the beginning. Our grandmother Moira McKenna was what the Irish call fey."

"You mean she had premonitions?"

"Among other gifts. She could communicate with animals. She could heal people—"

"Heal as in a doctor?"

Not having seen her ability for himself, he hedged, "Of a sort."

"A folk doctor?"

"You could call it that." She had used homegrown herbs, after all. "Her talents weren't always appreciated," Neil went on. "But different aspects of her gifts were inherited by most of her nine grandchildren. Actually, all of her grandchildren except for Skelly. He has to make do with her love of storytelling."

"Except...that means that you got one of these gifts."

"I didn't think so," he muttered, wondering how he was now discussing something so awkward for him with a stranger. "But I recently found out differently."

"How? Did you look into some tea leaves and realize you were able to read them?"

The sudden amusement in her tone set him further on edge. "Nothing so innocent. I touched someone and saw something that happened to her later."

"So that's the legacy? That you see things before they happen?"

"Partly. What it really means—or so my sister and cousins insist—is finding both love and danger together within thirty-three days of our thirty-third birthdays."

There, he'd said it, as stupid as that had sounded...

"And you just turned thirty-three." Annabeth sank into silence for a moment before murmuring, "Love and danger. Well, I guess the danger part already came true."

"Only it isn't over."

"What do you mean?"

"I had another vision similar to the first. It hasn't happened to her yet."

"Her?"

"You."

"What!"

He could feel her glare at him in the dark. "That was my reaction."

"You expect me to believe that you saw what happened to us today ahead of time like...like some paranormal broadcast?"

Her sudden indignation was catching.

"Not exactly! I didn't really know what I was seeing. When you were on your way to Wainwright, I tried to stop you and *that's* when it happened. The vision stopped me cold in my tracks and hit me like a freight train. You were terrified, eyes wide, licking your lips," he said, remembering. "A trickle of sweat trailed down the side of your face, and I could hear your heart pounding..." He snapped his gaze to hers. "I saw and felt what you were going through. Twice!" he insisted.

Her eyes were wide now. He could see them even though the only illumination in the car came from the streetlight.

"You're serious?"

"Never more."

They stared at each other for a moment. Then she shook her head, muttering, "This is ridiculous," and reached for the door handle.

"Don't you want to know what else I saw?"

She froze, her fingers inches from the handle. "All right. What?"

"You on some deserted city street. Terrified. Not alone."

"Oh, great, feed into a woman's biggest fear."

"I'm only telling you what I saw."

"When?"

"When Nickels grabbed your arm. He linked us together. I think he was the man in the vision."

"That's it!" She grasped the handle.

Not done yet, he grasped her arm.

A high-voltage connection…sending him spinning into the void of the future…

Palpable fear passes between them.

He's with Annabeth, holding her, feeling the feed of her pulse beneath his palms.

"Neil…"

She fairly breathes his name and the soft sound stirs the short hairs at the back of his neck.

"Shh, it's all right now."

"No, he knows where I am…he can get to me at any time…"

"But I'm here with you," he soothes. "You're not alone."

"Not alone," she echoes.

Her wide-open blue eyes swim with unwept emotion.

Then she touches him. A gentle stroke, her fingers

flutter to the side of his face. He sighs and does something unexpected, turns his head so that his lips touch her fingers, then her open palm.

"Neil…"

"Annabeth…"

Their mouths hover only centimeters apart.

Her fear beats against him now, her heart drums a message to his. They're breasts to chest, hip to hip, lips to lips. He claims her. Everything she knows and feels is his.

Odd how terror turns to raging desire…

Chapter Five

Abruptly thrown back to the present and the cramped front seat of the truck, Neil sensed discomfort along with the pleasure of having his lips locked over softer ones. In his arms, Annabeth sighed into his mouth and opened hers slightly.

An invitation to enter, Neil thought, one that he couldn't resist.

Hazily, slipping his tongue into the warm crevice, he tried to figure out what had just happened even as he thoroughly explored her mouth, and the kiss went on and on and on.

Suddenly Annabeth gasped and shoved at his chest. "What do you think you're doing?"

It took him a moment to blink back into his conscious mind. "Same as you, I guess."

"I didn't kiss you!"

"Damned if you didn't."

"Not first."

"Just the same."

"Well...stop it!" Annabeth whirled toward the door and jerked the handle.

Neil muttered, "Trust me, Sunshine, you weren't wanting me to stop anything."

With a frustrated-sounding shriek, she forced the door open. Even as she slid from the passenger seat, Neil got out on his side.

"I hope you don't think you're coming in," she said, nearly jogging down the sidewalk, as if she wanted to get away from him as quickly as possible.

He stalked her, saying, "I'm walking you to the door."

All the while keeping tabs on the neighborhood. One kiss hadn't knocked him senseless. He peered in every direction, into every shadow, aware of potential risks, especially when they started down the dark gangway.

But no danger met them...this time.

Annabeth lived behind a fancy old Victorian. The former coach house had been turned into a garage with a studio apartment above. Not that he'd seen it for himself. She had told him about it when he'd delivered her to change for the party. Since there hadn't been a parking spot available, he'd pulled the truck next to the fireplug then, as well, and had waited there while she'd cleaned up.

And she'd cleaned up right nicely, he thought.

"Your coming any farther really isn't necessary, Neil. I can see myself in."

They were crossing the backyard now. The space was softly lit, so he could make out a patio with flower borders and a tree for shade. No place for anyone to hide, he thought. At least that was something.

"Seeing you to your actual door will make me feel

better,'' he insisted. ''Indulge me until I know for sure that you're out of danger.''

''The police will take care of the situation.''

''Maybe. Eventually. But until then, I'll make sure you're okay.''

''Until then?'' That stopped her cold. She whirled on him. ''What are you planning on doing?'' she demanded to know. ''Camping out front in your truck every night?''

He was standing over her, wanting to kiss her again. Wanting to stir a little fire in her so that she would ask him inside.

Instead, he kept his arms pinned to his sides and his voice even. ''I'm no masochist. I'm just going to wait until you're inside with your door locked.''

''And it locks well,'' she muttered, setting off again. She headed right up the stairs that ran alongside the old coach house. ''*Two* dead bolts.''

''I'm impressed.''

When she opened the door, Neil got a quick glimpse inside. A big, high-ceiling room. Not much furniture. Bright colors. Lots and lots of plants.

Annabeth held out her hand and shoved it at him. ''Thanks. Nice meeting you, despite the circumstances.''

Neil took the proffered hand and admired her shake. Firm. No-nonsense. Not one of those limp-fingered deals that some women seemed to think were expected of them. Those non-handshakes drove him nuts.

''Goodbye, Neil.''

Reluctantly, he let go of her hand. ''Not goodbye,

Annabeth, but good night. I promise you haven't seen the last of me.''

She opened her mouth as if to squawk some rebuttal, then abruptly clamped her jaw shut, flew inside and locked the dead bolts.

Both of them.

On the way back to his truck, Neil couldn't help smiling. Until he analyzed what was happening to him.

Love and danger...The McKenna Legacy...his turn...act selflessly in another's behalf, and my legacy will be yours...

Was it possible?

Was Annabeth Caldwell the one?

That one powerful kiss had certainly made it seem so.

And yet, she wasn't right for him. She was too impulsive, too outspoken. Neil wanted a woman who could make life comfortable. Which made the rest even more difficult. The stuff that came hand in hand with the legendary attraction. Danger. Lives in peril. His. Hers.

Neil shook his head.

Unacceptable. But also ungovernable.

He had no real choices here. Though he might like to walk away from the situation—from the insanity that could mean lives—he couldn't. For with his grandmother's good wishes for him came obligation.

And if there was one thing Neil understood, it was the core meaning of being responsible. Sometimes, he thought being so damn dependable was the curse of his life.

His mood darkened.

He would dread what came next until it actually happened.

If family history were any indicator, he wouldn't have long to wait. Until then, until he met his real fate, he would be looking over his shoulder, checking every shadow. And to that same end, he had to insinuate himself into Annabeth's life as quickly as possible so that when trouble came, he would be around to shield her.

Act selflessly in another's behalf, his grandmother had invited.

Letter or not, he would do it anyway because he kept getting negative glimpses of her future. He would do it because he had to. Maybe that made him foolish, but he didn't know any other way to be.

As Neil rounded the truck, his mood soured further. For something was flapping from the driver's-door window.

A parking ticket!

He ripped it from the window, climbed into the truck and turned on the overhead light so he could read it.

Damn! That walk to Annabeth's door had just cost him a hundred dollars.

Stuffing the ticket in the glove compartment, he started the engine and headed for home. Rather, Skelly's home, where he would be lucky to sleep past daylight. If he didn't wake on his own, the triplets would be all over him.

In any case, the morning would come too soon for him, Neil thought, because whether or not he liked it—whether or not *she* liked it—he would have to insert himself in Annabeth's life. And he knew exactly how to approach her, at least to start. He would get a new draw, and it was his right as a contestant to go check on his calf.

Assuming this one wasn't missing.

PROMISE OR THREAT?

As she headed across the rodeo grounds early the next morning, Annabeth couldn't stop thinking about Neil's last words to her before she'd slammed the door in his face.

She hadn't seen the last of him.

Why did that bother her so much? she wondered. Why was she experiencing a sense of anticipation that did nothing more than aggravate her?

Entering the barn, she saw Lloyd, for some reason rearranging the calves. He was shooing a couple of critters into the empty pen.

She cleared her throat and sang out, "Morning, Lloyd!"

He started and whipped around. "Annabeth, honey, didn't expect to see you here this early."

"I told you I would make it up to you. I figured you would need help this morning, so here I am."

"So you are." He swung the gate closed and hooked it. "But you're scheduled to work the chutes this evening, and I'm really gonna need you then."

If she didn't know better, she would think he didn't want her around. Her stomach clenched. Surely he wasn't thinking of firing her for going off to the police station the day before. She needed this job.

"I don't have anything else on my dance card for today," she said, trying to sound upbeat. "I can fill in wherever."

"That makes for a really long day," Lloyd argued. Then suddenly, he softened. "But, heck, I am short-handed. And I imagine you could use the extra pay. If you're sure—"

"I'm sure," she said, sagging inside. Relief turned her bones to jelly.

Lloyd grinned at her. "All right, then."

"Great!"

She needed to work not only for the money, but to keep her mind occupied. Spending hour upon hour alone after what had happened the day before would be too much for her to bear. She lived inside her head too much already.

"Can you handle things alone in here?"

"Absolutely."

Lloyd dusted off his hands. "Good. Good. I got some other problems to attend to."

"I'll be fine," she said to his back as he headed for the outside doors.

Mind-numbing, backbreaking work was just the thing to make her feel better.

ANNABETH CALDWELL—that's one name he would never forget. If not for her, he would be significantly richer this morning. Because of her, he'd forfeited the winnings of the biggest gamble of his life.

He strode the south end of the rodeo grounds and mourned the loss of what had to be a couple hundred thousand dollars. Sufficient cash to set him up in style.

But enough about the money. His freedom sang a torch song in his head, as if it was kissing him good-bye.

Not if he could help it.

The main thing linking him to a jail cell was working inside that barn. He didn't leave loose ends, not when he could help it. Annabeth Caldwell had to be silenced before she could bring judgment down on him.

Plotting how to get to her, *where* to get to her, he was stopped cold by the unexpected arrival of the Lone Ranger, who slipped inside the barn as fast as greased lightning.

What the hell was he doing here, anyhow?

Of course—he was there to see Annabeth.

Her name burned into his brain like wildfire. But it wouldn't be niggling at him for long. Once he figured out how to tie up this particularly irritating loose end, he could forget that she had ever existed at all.

HAVING JUST DISTRIBUTED a large bag of feed, Annabeth felt the short hairs at the back of her neck stand to attention and knew she wasn't alone. Heart thumping, gut clenching, she whipped around to face Neil Farrell.

"What are you doing here?" she demanded, suddenly weak-kneed. He'd practically scared her to death, not that she would admit as much.

"Looking for a calf."

"Sorry. Casper hasn't shown up that I know of."

He waggled a slip of paper at her. "New draw."

"Oh, well, help yourself."

"Don't mind if I do."

After checking the slip, Neil found the right pen and did a cursory search for the calf.

Despite herself, caught by his rugged good looks and whipcord-hard body, Annabeth watched for a moment.

"There you are, fella," he said, gazing at the critter whose entire face was white. "Or should I call you Ronaldo?"

And for another moment, she remembered the delicious pleasure of being drawn up against that body, of having her mouth invaded so boldly. Her lips tingled with the memory.

Suddenly she realized that Neil seemed to be staring at her mouth rather than at his draw.

"Why are you *really* here?" she asked softly, turning back to her work so that he couldn't read her.

"The calf isn't enough reason?"

"I just...just..." The spell wore off now that she wasn't looking at him. "Just don't believe it, is all."

"All right. I admit it. I'm checking on you. I wanted to make sure you were okay. That do it for you?"

That did it, all right. That made her mad.

Scowling, she turned back to him. "I'm not a child, Neil."

"I can see that."

When he flicked his gaze over her, he made her squirm inside. "Keep your eyes in your head," she admonished him.

"I'd rather keep them on you."

The double meaning of his statement both flattered and put her off. He was attracted to her. And she'd be lying to herself if she tried to pretend the feeling wasn't mutual. But the deeper meaning, the *take-care-of* implication, didn't sit well with her.

Having taken care of herself for several years now, Annabeth resented Neil's interference. Even if his intentions were the best, she didn't need him.

She didn't need a bodyguard.

She didn't need anyone.

"If you're done looking," she snapped, "I have work to do."

"I'm not stopping you."

"You're distracting me."

"*Am* I?" He lifted one eyebrow.

"Don't flatter yourself. I meant you're annoying."

"Annoying how?"

"Like a barn fly I'd like to go after with a swatter."

"I get to you that much, do I?"

Exasperated, Annabeth clenched her jaw and crossed her arms over her chest. Whatever she said somehow managed to sound like something else. Something more intimate. At least Neil loved to interpret her that way.

"Just go," she said through gritted teeth.

"Only if you promise to meet me for lunch."

"I already have plans," she hedged.

Right, she'd planned on joining her co-workers in the mess tent for a big meal. She hadn't had much of an appetite at the party the night before. And while that stick-to-her-ribs bowl of oatmeal had done the trick early this morning, her stomach was already growling.

"How about dinner?"

"I'll be busy."

"I didn't name a time."

"So name it," she said.

"Six."

"Busy."

"Seven, then."

"Busy."

"What about five?"

"Busy. And you have a ride in the calf-roping event this evening anyway. Ronaldo will be waiting for you."

"If I didn't know better, I would think you were trying to avoid me."

Annabeth clamped her jaw shut. Sometimes less was better, especially around Neil Farrell.

"I will be seeing you around," he promised, suddenly so serious that a chill crawled up Annabeth's spine.

Now she figured he was going to start in on the visions again. She didn't know if he was being straight with her or not. Maybe he did see things. Maybe his whole family did. A family of lunatics. No, that wasn't fair. The McKennas weren't any crazier than anyone else's family. Maybe Neil's story was gospel. Or maybe he was telling tall tales to keep her in line. To control her. Believing *that* was preferable to believing in visions of doom.

"If you're going to spout some kind of warning again…save your breath, okay?"

"I just want to make sure you're safe."

"Well, you can't. No one can make sure any one else is safe." A sudden image of her father in a coffin caught her by surprise. "Our fates are already set." And her brother. She'd tried to save Larry and had failed miserably. "It's no use fighting."

"You really believe that?"

"I've got the scars to prove it."

Not literal scars, perhaps, but on the inside.

"Then why did you try to make a break for it?" Neil asked. "Yesterday, you took an active part in ending the hostage situation."

"I—I was afraid." And angry. "I wasn't thinking. I told you that."

"But you changed things. Fate had nothing to do with it. If you had just left well enough alone, things might have worked out very differently. So I guess your trying to get away was a good thing."

Annabeth gaped. He certainly had changed his tune. She didn't know how to respond to that. Neil was correct, of course. For once, something she had done may have had some positive effect on the outcome of her situation.

A first time for everything, she guessed.

Neil backed off toward the barn door. "Later, Annabeth, come see me ride."

She didn't tell him that she would be working the arena that night.

Nor that he would be hard to miss.

NEIL FOUND SKELLY at the pony ride late that afternoon, as planned. The timed events would start soon.

The rest of the family was there, as well. The triplets and Keelin's little girl were on ponies and half the adults were accompanying them, and the other half stood close enough to watch.

"How goes it, cuz?" Skelly asked as he moved away from the group toward Neil.

"I'm ready to ride." Neil pulled an envelope from his pocket and handed it to Skelly. "Here are those tickets I promised you."

The whole family would be in the audience to see him compete in the first round. Nothing like adding pressure to the one thing that usually relaxed him.

"I didn't mean the competition," Skelly said. "I was referring to Miss Annabeth."

"She's not exactly charmed by me."

"Really? Sounds…interesting."

"What?"

Skelly arched an eyebrow. "Well, if things went too smoothly, you'd be bored."

Neil shook his head. Why couldn't things go smoothly? Why couldn't a man—he—be attracted to a peaceful, agreeable woman. One who was not Annabeth Caldwell? Life would be so simple.

When he was around Annabeth, Neil didn't know what got into him. No other woman had ever affected him in quite this way. Annabeth challenged him to use wit rather than logic with her, and yes, subterfuge rather than his normal straightforward approach.

"So what's been going on?" Skelly asked. "Anything suspicious? Any more visions?"

"Thankfully, no."

The one of him and Annabeth in a hot embrace

didn't count. Not that Skelly wouldn't appreciate those details. Neil just wasn't ready to share them.

"If I were you, I would be looking over my shoulder. And Miss Annabeth's. Not exactly an onerous task."

"She's not taking any of this seriously," Neil complained. "She talks about fate as if it can't be changed."

"It can't, at least not like you think. I believe we're given forks in the road, varied opportunities. An open mind helps us to choose the right ones," Skelly said. "Like women who are right for us."

"There you have it, then," Neil said. "Annabeth isn't right for me at all."

"How do you know for certain if you haven't tried her?" Skelly's eyebrow arched at him.

A private man, Neil was somewhat aghast that his entire family was watching his every move with Annabeth, anticipating some kind of legacy-union. What a man and woman shared should be for themselves alone. Period.

"Sex isn't everything," he groused.

"Now, who said anything about sex?" Skelly asked. "You must have it—or the lack thereof—on your mind. What I meant was that a man has to try on a woman to see if she fits him, fills in all the missing spaces in his life. She has to be able to keep him on his toes, keep him guessing about her intentions. Just plain keep him interested."

Annabeth certainly qualified for all of the above, Neil thought uneasily. If Skelly was right...

Then she was in big trouble for sure.

Chapter Six

"C'mon, move along, little dogies," Annabeth sing-songed as she and a grizzled stock laborer named Jake herded two dozen calves from the barn to the holding pen directly behind the north end of the roofed arena. She whistled and yelled, "Get moving, you slackers! Yee-ha!"

"Think you're in a real roundup, do you?" muttered Jake.

But as he turned away, Annabeth caught the grin spreading beneath his droopy mustache.

"Yeah, I've always wanted to be a cowboy," she teased. "Riding the range, chewing tobacco, telling tall tales at the campsite."

"You'd make a good one." He grinned wider. "Boys would like you right fine."

The temporary alleyway of piped rail was sectioned off so that the critters moved along a bit at a time, from one pen to another. Jake was working the forward gates, opening them, and Annabeth was pushing the calves through and closing the gate behind them. That way, they couldn't change their minds and try to head back for the barn. The quick and efficient system was used to move all stock, from calves to bulls.

The small herd was charging through the last section, when Annabeth sensed someone behind her.

Whipping around, she spotted Alderman Salvador Lujan, his dark eyes pinned to her. He was barely ten feet from where she stood. Expecting he was going to lay into her as he had the day before, she was creeped out when he bared his teeth in a fake smile and simply walked away.

Annabeth rubbed the gooseflesh from her arms and closed the gate behind the herd.

What had *that* been all about?

She didn't have long to think on it before Lloyd appeared. "I need one of the other boys that I assigned here to work as a flank man in roughstock. He needs to go pick a mount and tack up. So Jake will push the calves through from here and you'll have to handle the arena chute yourself."

"No problem," she said, glancing over her shoulder to check for the alderman.

But the coast was clear.

"You're doing a fine job, Annabeth. You seem to have gotten over what happened to us pretty smoothly."

"Haven't you?" She checked out Lloyd a little more closely. Tension rather than the usual laugh lines radiated from his eyes behind the metal frames. "Are you all right?"

"Yeah, sure. That was one hell of a bad deal, though."

Especially for the man who died, she thought, though she didn't voice that opinion.

Instead, she said, "None of the hostages got hurt, thankfully."

"No, not yet."

"What do you mean?"

Lloyd just shrugged and patted her shoulder. "Forget it. Next week it'll seem like a bad dream."

"Dreams fade. I'll never forget a single detail about what happened yesterday."

Sobering further, Lloyd nodded and moved away. "You just keep on doing your usual fine job."

Wondering what was troubling the stock contractor, Annabeth left the calves to Jake and slipped inside the arena.

She couldn't help but wonder about the dead man though. Had the police identified him? Had they gotten any leads on the man whose description she gave them? Had there been any progress on the case at all?

Between events, one of the specialty acts was performing. Three riders were racing at top speed around the arena. In sync, they popped up, placed booted feet on their saddles, and within seconds stood atop their mounts with arms fully extended. The Hippodrome Stand was a classic, as was their next move, the Cossack Drag, in which they dropped down, heads hanging to the ground close to the flying horse hooves.

Knowing the act was almost over, she glanced behind the chute and roping box.

Cowboys were checking their horses' tack and their gear—looped ropes and the pigging strings that they'd hold in their mouths until it was time to tie up the calves' legs. She wasn't actually looking for Neil, she told herself as her gaze swept along until she found him.

While most of the competitors seemed tense—she'd caught several indulging in some superstitious good-luck rituals—Neil Farrell was the picture of relaxed. She hadn't seen him this loose since she'd met him. His Stetson was pushed back, exposing his high forehead. His eyes had a dreamy quality, as if he were on some other planet where only good things happened to people like them.

The reminder of her own troubles turned her back to the arena just as the specialty act ended.

Annabeth clapped along with the audience, then moved the first calf into place and took her position at the chute gate.

While everyone settled in for the event, she took a quick look around to see if Lujan was somewhere in the audience, staring at her, but if the alderman was watching, he was lost in the crowd.

Looped rope in hand, six-foot pigging string also looped and clenched in his teeth, the first competitor backed his horse into the roping box and then settled behind the rope barrier. A moment later he nodded to Annabeth and she released the calf. The little critter flew forward, taking his lead, the tie around his neck releasing when it hit twenty feet.

As his tightly wound horse shot out of the box and through the barrier, the cowboy swung the loop over his head and cast it around the calf's neck. The horse braked, the cowboy hit the dust and the line between saddle horn and calf went taut. The cowboy ran along the line, grabbed the calf by the head and flank and threw him, then trussed three of his legs together. Eight-point-three seconds. A good time.

But then before the cowboy could remount his horse, the calf struggled to his feet, ruining the man's chances for this round, at least.

Moving the second calf into position, Annabeth thought that at least the competition gave all the contestants a fair shot at some winnings. While there was money on the line each night, the big prizes came on the last night. Each calf roper had to compete in five of seven rounds over the course of the week. Scores were cumulative. On that last night, then, the five competitors with the top scores would have a showdown.

Bringing herself back to today's competition, Annabeth waited for the calf roper's nod.

The second run was successful, if slower.

"Nine-point-one seconds for Colt Adams!" came the announcement from the booth directly behind the calf chute and over the loudspeakers.

Annabeth spotted Neil's family huddled together in two rows in a nearby section of the grandstand. The toddlers perched on adults' laps, their little faces painted with clown makeup. When Jane waved, it took Annabeth a moment to realize the wave was for her. She waved back as the next contestant settled in place.

"Next up, a cowboy from Coyote, New Mexico…Bill Hamilton!"

The competition had a rhythm of its own. Most rides went smoothly, many times were under nine seconds. One calf rolled and the roper had to right it. He went over thirteen seconds. Another roper missed the calf altogether and couldn't get it back. He left the arena one angry and embarrassed cowboy.

And then Neil was up on his bay, Cisco. His wolf gaze burned into her until her palms began to sweat. He gave her the nod. She released the calf.

Watching him was like watching poetry in motion. The way he leaned forward in the saddle, at one with Cisco, loop roiling overhead. The throw...the horse braking, forelegs straight...Neil bounding to the ground...all went so smoothly that Annabeth caught herself holding her breath.

Neil trailed the taut rope, flanked Ronaldo and tied up his legs. He threw up his hands and smoothly remounted.

"Seven-point-nine seconds, ladies and gentlemen," the announcer called, all full of enthusiasm. *"Neil Farrell has taken the lead!"*

An explosion of applause burst from the audience.

And Annabeth felt an unexpected swell of pleasure, no doubt due to the fact that she actually knew the man, she told herself. Nothing more.

Still, she couldn't help grinning as she lined up the next calf.

Three competitors to go. The first couldn't get the calf's legs together properly fast enough. Eleven-point-seven seconds.

The next contestant waited too long to throw the noose. Thirteen-point-two seconds.

The third did his job smoothly. Seven-point-six seconds.

Three-tenths of a second faster than Neil, Annabeth thought, disappointment filling her.

"La-a-adies and gentlemen, your winner of the first round of the calf-roping competition...Ty-y-yler Grant! C'mon and give Ty a big hand."

As the audience cheered, Annabeth looked back in the readying area for Neil. He was loosening his horse's cinch, appearing for all the world as if he hadn't a care. Any other man beaten so close would probably react somehow—throw his hat down or at least cuss a little. But Neil seemed as relaxed as he had at the beginning of the competition.

Because he figured he would make up the time in coming rounds?

Or because he just didn't care about winning?

Impressed either way, Annabeth thought to talk to him. She wanted to tell him what a great run he'd had, how much she'd enjoyed watching him, how disappointed she was for him. He had, after all, invited her to watch.

But before she could get back to the readying area, he'd done a disappearing act.

Inexplicably disappointed, she turned back to the holding pen where the calves awaited a return trip to the barn. She threw herself into her work and vanquished a certain South Dakota cowboy from her mind.

"I HEAR YOU were counseling Annabeth last night."

Neil broached the subject with his cousin Curran's wife as they trailed the group through the night across the brightly lit festival grounds. Curran being deep into a spirited discussion with his sister, Keelin, Neil had decided to keep Jane company. The late hour had been too much for the little kids, so the adults had decided to leave before cranky progressed to screaming-tired.

"I wasn't counseling her, exactly." Jane grinned at him. "Just letting her in on some of the facts of being in a relationship with a McKenna man."

"We're not in a relationship."

"Not yet, perhaps—"

"*Not* being the significant word here." Neil insisted, "She's not my type." No matter that he was attracted to her anyway.

"Perfect, then."

Through gritted teeth, he said, "I just plan on seeing to her safety in any way I can, is all."

"You keep telling yourself that."

Why did the members of his family treat him like an idiot? Neil wondered.

When he carried through with his plan for the evening, they would be convinced they were right, of course, but he would know better. He clenched and unclenched his jaw. Tried to relax. He'd been thinking on The McKenna Legacy—actually, he'd been doing little else since he and Annabeth had been thrown together—and his obligation was clear. He needed to keep her safe from danger.

That didn't mean he automatically had to make Annabeth Caldwell his woman.

Bits of that last vision—the one that had led up to the knee-melting kiss in the truck—flitted through his mind, but he brushed that away. He *did* have control over his own actions, at least.

"So what's the plan?" Jane asked.

"To stick close by Annabeth's side until this thing is resolved."

"You're going to get a job as a stock laborer?"

"Not exactly. I figure she's safe enough once she's here on the grounds with all the people around."

"Just as she was when you were taken hostage yesterday morning?"

A point that Neil ignored. "The vision of danger that I had—it didn't happen here. It was in some other neighborhood, maybe even *her* neighborhood. She doesn't live too far from one of those elevated lines on the rapid-transit system. Though I don't know how the bastard would find her. Thankfully, Detective Wexler kept his word—Annabeth's name wasn't released to the media." He'd double-checked both major papers and various news programs on local channels to be certain.

"Ah, so you're going to keep watch over her *at home?*"

Jane looked so smug that Neil enjoyed saying, "I'm merely going to see her home at night and pick her up for work in the morning."

"And if your schedules don't coincide?"

"They'll just have to. Besides, with that composite of Nickels that she helped shape for the police, it won't be long before the thief is picked up."

"I do hope you're right," Jane said, the teasing in her voice suddenly vanquished.

"Right about what?" Skelly asked, dropping back from the group to join them.

"About the police wrapping up the case quickly," Jane said.

They'd reached a crossroads near the food stalls. Just ahead, his family could flag down a couple of taxis. Neil would go back to find Annabeth for that ride home. Odors of cooked food assailed him and his stomach growled in protest. He was hungry again.

He was just wondering if he could persuade Annabeth to get something to eat, when Skelly said, "Take care of Miss Annabeth," and swatted Neil in the arm.

"How do you know that I'm going to see her?" Skelly hadn't, after all, been in on the conversation with Jane.

Skelly merely arched an eyebrow. "If you need backup, cuz, sound the alarm."

"I don't think it will come to that."

"And don't keep the lady up too late." Donovan moved in to stick in his two cents. "Your Annabeth might not need any beauty rest, but tomorrow is a workday for her."

"I'm just going to see her home. That's it," Neil insisted, abruptly changing plans about getting some chow, deciding he could raid the refrigerator when he got back to Skelly's place.

"Go on with you, now," Curran said, his arm around Jane's waist. "And be looking over your shoulder, lad. You'll not know from which direction the danger will commence."

His cousins and their mates all gave him like advice as they said their goodbyes. Curran and Jane would be going back to Kentucky at daybreak. And Donovan and Laurel would likewise be leaving for Wisconsin.

That still left enough McKennas around to keep him irritated, Neil figured.

Waving his family off, he headed back across the grounds to find Annabeth and offer her that ride home.

BY THE TIME she was through rustling calves and was ready to head for home, Annabeth was exhausted. The day had been long, the work hard. She would sleep well that night.

Darkness already awaited her.

To her left, the cityscape glowed in electric splendor, as did the festival's midway straight ahead on the other side of the arena. While rides and food booths and the music stages wouldn't shut down until Grant Park closed for the night, the actual rodeo was already winding up. Drifting from the arena came audience reactions as a clown bullfighter kept spectators on the edge of their seats.

Yawning, Annabeth started to leave the area, then decided that using a Porta Pottie before heading for public transportation would be in her best interest. The portable toilets stood along the curb, next to the blocked-off street turned parking lot for the stock trucks and horse vans and vehicles of festival workers and contestants.

At the moment, however, only the row of portable toilets stood sentinel over the parking lot like silent soldiers. Pools of light from the street lamps limned the structures that reminded her of upright coffins.

The area was majorly deserted.

Everyone within hearing distance was probably jammed into the arena, glued to the antics of some grown man who was crazy enough to put on a clown suit and makeup and dance directly in front of a raging bull.

Just the thought of putting oneself in such peril made Annabeth shiver, but everyone had his or her own danger threshold, she guessed, her mood darkening now that she didn't have work to occupy her.

The portable toilets were already rank, so she got in and out as quickly as she could.

Then, yawning again, tired eyes watering, she washed her hands at the portable sink that stood before the row of Porta Potties.

Some low noise competing with the trickling water raised her hackles. Hands wet, she froze and concentrated. The sound—the clack of boot heels against pavement?—came from directly behind her.

Before she could turn around to see who was there, rough hands shoved her forward onto the sink.

"Hey—"

Her head was smacked into the faucet and for a brief moment she saw stars.

"Don't move," a low, hoarse voice commanded as internal stars lit her mind. "Don't turn around."

A large hand gripped the back of her neck hard to make certain she couldn't disobey. Another hand searched her intimately, making her stomach clench and her gorge rise while the rest of her seemed to freeze.

As much as she might want to, she couldn't seem to move. She couldn't fight.

Then the hand slipped into her side pocket.

Her wallet!

Dear Lord, her paycheck!

Getting her wits about her, Annabeth struggled and yelled, "No! You can't—"

But obviously he could. She felt the leather lift free of her pocket. This couldn't be happening to her. Not one more bad thing! She screamed and kicked backward, but all her running shoe met was air.

"Let go!"

"What's going on over there?" someone shouted from a distance.

Though the voice was familiar, Annabeth couldn't get a handle on it, for she was struggling with the thief, trying to break his grip. Somehow he'd managed to slip his hand around the front of her neck. She clawed at the fingers of steel to no avail.

They tightened perceptibly.

Air! She needed air!

Even as she struggled to get some, her attacker whirled her back toward the portable toilets. Knees weak, she stumbled along, still doing her best to break his grip. Those stars behind her eyes were shining brighter now and her lungs felt ready to burst when he finally released her.

Gasping, throwing out her hands for something to steady herself, Annabeth teetered forward.

Her attacker gave her a hard shove in the middle

of her back and she went flying. Then a horrible odor and the edge of something hard against her knees stopped her.

"No!" she rasped, twisting around just as the Porta Pottie door shut and was latched from the outside.

Trapped in a disgusting outhouse!

"Help!" she squeaked, jiggling the release futilely. Then, gathering enough spit to swallow, she tried again. "Somebody help me!"

She hit the door of the unit with the flat of her hands. The walls around her shook but the door didn't budge.

"Annabeth? Is that you?"

"Neil? Get me out of here!"

"Where are you?"

She banged some more. "Here. I'm in this hot, stinking hole!" Sweat was trickling down her spine and beads of moisture dotted her all over. Trying to breathe only through her mouth, keeping her nose blocked, she gasped, "Some guy attacked me and locked me in!"

Adrenaline and the stench both working on her, Annabeth only hoped he hurried before she was sick.

"Bang again so I can find you!"

She did, the action jolting her already upset stomach.

"There you are."

"Hurry!" she pleaded, trying to hold her breath as the latch rattled.

"Hang in there," Neil said. "I just...have to get this...free. Got it."

So did she.

Even as the door swung open on creaky hinges, Annabeth's stomach gave up the ghost and she heaved its contents all over Neil Farrell's cowboy boots.

Chapter Seven

Neil caught Annabeth by the shoulders and steadied her as she was sick. Looking down at the mess splashing his boots, he winced but didn't say a word.

"I'm sorry," she gasped, covering her mouth with a hand that trembled. "Didn't mean to do that. I—I was shaky and th-then, when he locked me in that disgusting hole—"

"Whoa, no need to apologize."

Neil thought to pull Annabeth close and comfort her, but even though she looked vulnerable and in need of a pair of strong arms to steady her, something kept him from doing it. Holding her seemed like a dangerous venture. Probably the ongoing debate with his family kept him from following his own instincts, Neil thought wryly.

Reaching into his pocket, he pulled out a cotton bandanna. "Here."

"Thanks," she said, taking it from him.

"Are you all right?"

Dabbing at her mouth, she nodded. "I am now that you're here, except..." Her eyes suddenly pooled. "My wallet—the creep got my wallet!"

"But he didn't get *you,* did he? He didn't hurt you?"

Yet another of life's little ironies, Neil realized—he'd just assured Jane that Annabeth would be safe alone on the rodeo grounds.

She said, "Just my head when he banged it into the faucet."

"Let me see."

Neil pulled her around so the streetlight hit her face. Steeling himself against the physical sensation such a simple touch evoked—and that instinct that made him want to take her in his arms and reassure her—he smoothed the pale hair back from her forehead. A slight shadow was beginning to mar her hairline.

"What's the prognosis, Doc?" she joked, a slight quiver in her voice.

"You'll live." He stared into her eyes to make certain both pupils were evenly dilated. No concussion that he could tell. "A little bruised but it doesn't look too bad."

"Well, we have something in common, after all." Her blue eyes were wide on his face.

"Right. A few bruises." Souvenirs of his tussle with Nickels. "So, how much do yours hurt?"

"A couple of aspirin should do the job."

"Maybe someone should take a look at you."

"No doctors," she said firmly.

No doctors because she didn't need one or because she couldn't afford one?

"I was thinking of the paramedic team that's on the grounds in case someone gets gored or stomped."

"I'm fine," she insisted.

"All right. But if your head gets any worse, you *will* do something about it." Even if he had to throw her over his saddle and ride her to the medic station himself. "In the meantime, we should find you some ice to keep the swelling and bruising down."

"We should find my wallet and my paycheck!" Annabeth countered. "I couldn't get to the bank yesterday for obvious reasons. Now I won't have enough money to pay my rent. I suppose Lloyd could put a stop on that check and cut me another, assuming he could get to it in time before the bastard cashes the original."

Talk about living close to the vest. Neil wondered how in the world she had gotten herself into such financial trouble, until he remembered the list of jobs she'd recited. He guessed a person who kept switching jobs would have a hard time keeping up with expenses.

Suddenly looking down, she moaned. "Your boots. Oh, Neil, I really am sorry. Let's get you some water so you can clean them off."

Annabeth marched to the portable sink and wet his bandanna.

"You probably need the water more than I do," he said. "Any cups around here?"

"You think I'm going to drink out of this? Thanks, but I'd rather take my chances on finding a fountain with water fit for human consumption."

She had a point. So Neil took the wet bandanna from her and quickly wiped off his boots, then discarded the soiled material.

"C'mon, Sunshine, let's get you that ice."

He lightly set an arm around her back and guided her toward the midway. Everything in him told him to wrap that arm around her more fully and draw her close into his side. His fingers itched to track the curve of her waist, to tighten fast to her soft flesh.

Confused about what was happening to him, Neil resisted. He'd never before considered himself suggestible, but at the moment that's exactly what he feared. Things were all mixed up in his mind—his attraction to Annabeth and the danger she seemed to attract, his grandmother's legacy and the well-meaning counsel of his family.

He needed some downtime to sort it all out, but that wouldn't be now. Later, when he was alone, he would have time to think on it.

Approaching the food stands, he spotted one without a line and quickly had in hand a small plastic bag filled with ice cubes. He brushed Annabeth's hair from her forehead and placed the bag where the bruising was growing more evident.

"Hold the ice there for ten minutes or so, then you'll need to do it again later."

"Thanks."

"Now we'd better find a phone and call the police."

"And Lloyd."

And so they found themselves back in the press office, again empty. Thankful they were alone, Neil got a shaky Annabeth to sit. She didn't need a nosy reporter connecting this incident with what happened the day before. If it had been connected. He just didn't know.

He called 911 and reported the incident, then watched Annabeth closely.

Her skin appeared pale and she kept rubbing her arms as though she was cold. Not from the ice—she'd already set that down. Shock, Neil decided. He considered offering to get her something to drink, then thought better of it. He didn't want to leave her alone.

Suddenly she said, "Maybe it's me."

"What's you?"

"Bad luck. Bad karma. Whatever you want to call it. Maybe it's just me. If I hadn't gone looking for Lloyd yesterday, we wouldn't have been held hostage. And if I hadn't stopped in a deserted area tonight, some creep wouldn't have seen me as easy pickings and taken my wallet."

"Are you sure your attacker was simply after the wallet?"

"Well, it *is* gone. He filched it from my pocket, shoved me into the Porta Pottie and took off."

"No threats? He didn't say anything?"

"Like what? He just told me not to turn around," Annabeth said. "I'm sure that he didn't want me to be able to identify him in a lineup."

"Strange…"

"What? That he didn't want to get caught?"

"That two days in a row you were the victim of a thief who purposely hid his identity."

"I doubt any thief would want to be identified if he could get away without being seen. And this is the big city," she groused. "There's danger everywhere you turn. It's just a coincidence. Bad karma and more bad karma.''

But Neil wasn't so sure.

Her dark mood surprised him a bit. He was used to her being argumentative but in a different way. Like giving him a hard time. Now she was doing that to herself. Blaming herself. Or fate.

But wasn't that what The McKenna Legacy was all about—fate?

He didn't have long to think about it, for a moment later a uniformed policeman appeared. The dispatcher had contacted an officer already on the grounds. He took Annabeth's complaint but gave her little hope that her wallet or its contents would ever be returned.

Neil insisted that the patrolman forward a copy of the complaint to Detective Wexler, just in case there was any connection between the two incidents.

When the cop left, Annabeth sat there, stunned for a moment, then called Wainwright's answering service, left a message about the theft and then asked him to cancel the stolen paycheck and cut her another.

"I hope he can actually do something about it," she said despondently as she hung up.

Neil could tell the adrenaline was wearing off. Suddenly, she appeared nerveless, like a rag doll, as if she didn't have the energy to get herself out of there.

"Some hot food might be just the ticket," he said.

"Food," she echoed, shoving a hand into a pocket. When she pulled it free and opened her fist, two quarters, three dimes and a couple of pennies lay in her palm. "I don't even have money for a bus ride. I'll have to walk home."

"Not if I have anything to say about it. I'll take you home, of course. *After* we eat. And the meal is on me, too." Thinking she was going to refuse, he added, "I insist. I hate eating alone."

She blinked as if trying to keep from crying and nodded. "Thanks, Neil. I really appreciate it. So what are you in the mood for? Pizza or burgers?"

"I had something more substantial in mind."

Because he was a visitor to the city, he let her pick the place.

Down Home specialized in comfort food, meat loaf and mashed garlic potatoes—he was wary of something so exotic-sounding, but, after the first forkful, decided they were even better than his mother's homemade. Not that he would ever say so.

"I like this place," he said, looking around at the walls washed with deep color and the bric-a-brac in every nook. "It's comfortable, kind of like a home."

She grinned. "That's the idea, I guess."

The restaurant wasn't too crowded, but still a respectable number of customers for late Sunday night frequented the place. And because it wasn't one of those trendy places, the clientele was a mix—young, old and everything in between. Music played in the background. Soft rock that set a comfortable mood.

Gradually, the food and the atmosphere worked its magic on Annabeth, Neil noted with satisfaction. She seemed to be more like herself.

"I would just like to get my hands on that guy," she muttered threateningly, making a martial-arts hand gesture. "You know, face-to-face, when he doesn't have the element of surprise on his side."

Knowing she was just trying to make herself feel better—undoubtedly less vulnerable—Neil played along. "You'd take care of him, would you?"

"I'd give it my best shot."

"Karate?"

"Nah, just general self-defense. It's whatever works all mixed up. It was a couple-hour presentation at one of my jobs—I never had time to practice, actually. But I know I could have defended myself if the circumstances had been different."

Not really believing it, he asked, "So where did you learn to be so tough?"

"This city. It takes the life out of you if you let it. And sometimes when you don't."

Neil realized he was treading on personal territory when he asked, "Your family?"

"My father was strong and healthy when we moved here. That didn't stop him from dying in a construction accident. And then once Dad died, everything fell apart. Larry started acting out. My younger brother," she clarified, her expression darkening once more. "I guess he was looking for a father figure, someone to give him guidance. He just wouldn't believe that a gang leader didn't fit the bill."

"So he got into trouble."

She nodded. "Of the worst kind. The *fatal* kind. He was killed last spring…"

So that was the key, Neil thought. That's what she *hadn't* told him when they'd talked about family before.

Doubly tragic that her brother's death had spelled the real end of family for her. Undoubtedly her poor mother hadn't been able to deal with losing a son after losing her husband, and so had gone back to what she had seen as her safe roots in a small town.

But in doing so, she had left her daughter—an obviously vulnerable Annabeth—alone.

In an attempt to make her feel better, Neil said, "You can't blame your brother's death on yourself."

"Who said I did?" she snapped.

"All that talk about bad karma."

"Yeah, well..." Annabeth put on a too-bright expression. "Well, the good news is that you don't have to worry about me anymore."

"And that would be because...?"

"Your vision of me in danger...I came out all right. Well, in one piece anyway."

Neil almost let it ride. She was finding something positive to hold on to. But he couldn't let her fool herself.

"No, that wasn't it."

Her smile faded a tad. "I don't understand."

"Your getting mugged for your wallet on the rodeo grounds—that's not the danger I saw."

Neil would have liked to reassure her but it wasn't in his nature to lie.

Annabeth's smile disappeared. "You're saying there's more?" When Neil chose not to answer, she muttered, "Oh, great. Just great!" And shoved away the plate of half-eaten food. "I wouldn't mind getting out of here."

"I'll get the check."

"You know what—I can walk home from here."

"Don't be silly."

"No, you finish eating." Annabeth popped up out of her seat. "I'll see myself home. Thanks for dinner and the ride this far. And if Lloyd cuts that new check for me, I'll pay you back every penny."

Then, before Neil could stop her, she turned and headed for the door.

He had a bad feeling about this.

"Miss," he called to the waitress who was warming coffee several tables away. "Check, please. And hurry."

Neil rose and pulled out his wallet even as the young woman hurried over. He gave her far too much money but decided waiting for change would waste valuable time.

"Keep it all," he muttered, shoving his hat on his head and making his own escape.

Her surprised "Tha-a-ank you!" followed him as he charged toward the door.

Mere seconds later he flew onto the street. But it was already too late. Annabeth was nowhere in sight and he had no idea which direction she had taken. He didn't know the area.

What the hell was he supposed to do now?

The rumble of a nearby elevated train made him start. And the internal warning now threatening to consume him went straight from bad to worse.

ADRENALINE AND ANGER pushed Annabeth down the side street toward home. If she got any madder she would be talking to herself. Out loud. Then they could just put her away. Lock her up in a loony bin and throw away the key.

Yeah, she could see that happening, Annabeth thought. She could see anything bad happening in this city!

Or maybe it wasn't the city at all.

Maybe it was just *her* as she'd told Neil—bad, bad karma. Or maybe she hadn't tried hard enough to make things right.

Hadn't gotten Dad to take an easier job, one that wouldn't kill him.

Hadn't gotten her brother to cut off approaches by that gang leader who initiated him and led him to his death.

Hadn't gotten Mom to a better place psychologically so that she wouldn't abandon all hope—and *her*—to walk through life a living ghost.

Her fault...her fault...her fault...

The internal and too-familiar chant blended with the chatter of steel-on-steel overhead.

Clack-clack...clack-clack...clack-clack...

And with a too-familiar sound behind her.

A glance over her shoulder revealed nothing but her city-neighborhood street, dark and deserted, eerily lit. Two flats and three flats and old Victorians invaded by duplexes and condos and town houses, windows closed and shuttered against the all-seeing eyes in the night.

The screech of metal-on-metal made her jump. Over on the next block, the elevated train had come to a screeching halt to take on passengers.

A block from home. Now all she could hear was the distant drone of traffic. That and her own breath. And underneath both, something more sinister.

Footsteps?

She whirled around, danced backward, all the while piercing the dark with her frantic gaze.

Not a thing…not a thing…nothing…

Spooked anyway, she faced forward and moved faster. Less than a block. Who had she imagined would be there? Three-fourths of a block. Nickels? He couldn't know where she lived. The El train pulled away from the station.

Clack-clack…clack-clack…clack-clack…

The footsteps sharpened against the pavement. Was she imagining it or was this real? Half a block to go. Was someone really behind her, moving more swiftly, trying to catch up to her?

Glancing over her shoulder yet again, Annabeth gasped.

Nearly blending with the shadows, a big man followed, hunched over, covered head down, hands in pockets. Though he was wearing light clothing, he made a threatening silhouette.

With an explosion of breath, she ran. Less than quarter of a block to safety. The pulse of the train softened and now it was her heartbeat filling her ears.

Her mind raced faster than her feet.

What to do? What to do? How to get away?

What if she couldn't reach her apartment in time? *What if…what if…what if…?*

This was it. She'd had it! If she didn't take a stand, she would be defeated. Another victim. People murmuring regrets and then going on with their lives and forgetting. And who was there to remember?

The mother who'd left her?

Casual friends with busy lives?

Neil Farrell?

She had herself, Annabeth thought fiercely. She counted for something. And she was through running. Or would be once she arrived at the place where she would take her stand.

The courtyard between the main house and the carriage house awaited, the shadowy garden pooled in soft yellow light. She fled down the darkened gangway, already placing herself there mentally.

Lungs pumping, heart racing, she tried to calm herself. Prepare herself. Finding the tool she'd seen her elderly landlady Mrs. Kravitz use earlier, she grabbed it, slipped into the shadow of the big silver maple tree and waited for the man pursuing her.

The moment he so much as took one lousy step into the courtyard, Annabeth vowed she would make him sorry!

Jazzed, she lifted the shovel. Damn thing was heavy! But she was strong. Always had been. She just had to remember that. Had to remember that she could take on anything. Anyone. Standing with feet slightly spread, she balanced herself.

And waited…and waited…and waited…

Annabeth wasn't certain for how long before the weight of the heavy metal made her muscles burn with the strain. She listened hard and heard nothing. No footsteps. No scraping. No nothing.

Her lungs eased. Her heart slowed. She lowered the shovel and faced the truth.

The man hadn't been following her after all. She'd allowed Neil's dire predictions to spook her.

But still, the imagining had sparked something in her. A resolution. A vow that she would get control of her life, maybe for the first time ever.

She was through with believing everything would work out all right if only she were a decent person living a respectable life. That's what her parents had promised on the day they had all abandoned the farm and a way of life that she still mourned.

But now, unwilling to continue to sit back and wait for things to work out, Annabeth was determined to find a way to take her destiny into her own hands.

And then maybe she could stop being angry.

Stop being depressed.

Stop living without hope as her mother was so obviously doing.

Feeling better than she had in months, Annabeth set the shovel back where she'd found it, then moved from the shadows into the light.

Keys in hand, she swiftly crossed to her staircase, knowing that this day was a turning point in her life. She started up the steps. Distracted by the plans already forming in her mind, she didn't hear the footsteps behind her until it was almost too late.

Almost…

Whirling around, she kicked out and caught the man four steps below her in the chest. Pumped, she felt as if everything happened in slow motion—the man flying backward, her turning and dashing upward.

Her mental picture of him was shadowy and vague, but she knew it wasn't the man from the street. This one wore a ski mask, jeans and dark T-shirt.

Annabeth was almost to the door when she heard the man come after her. He tried wrapping an arm around her neck, but she shoved her chin down so that he couldn't get a good hold. Instinct drove her to clamp down on that beefy arm—with her teeth.

She bit down near his wrist as hard as she could.

He yelped. ''Bitch!''

Annabeth held on like a dog with a bone, her sharp teeth cutting through his flesh. When the metallic taste of blood startled her, she let go.

Praying that he didn't have a disease, she spit out the trace of blood in her mouth and scooted up a few more stairs before he caught up to her. Again she turned to fight him off, grabbing both railings so that she could kick him with both feet.

He ducked and she tried a second time.

Suddenly a large leather-gloved hand wrapped around one of her ankles. And a knife appeared in his other hand. Even as the fingers tightened so that she couldn't pull free, Annabeth kicked him again with her other foot, this time aiming for the knife and missing.

The knife was raised threateningly and she didn't see how he could miss her.

Frantic, she screamed for all she was worth.

Chapter Eight

Where the hell was she?

Neil practically jogged from his truck—legally parked this time—toward the old Victorian facing the carriage house. He'd driven up and down the side streets until he'd found one he recognized.

But Annabeth had vanished.

Heading down her gangway, Neil hoped she was safe in her own apartment.

The shrill of an elevated train competed with the shriek coming from behind the building. Neil ran, bursting free of the gangway in time to see a bizarre struggle on the carriage-house staircase. Annabeth was hanging on to the railings for dear life and kicking out at the man who held her fast by one ankle and was trying to stab her with a knife.

She screamed, "Let go of me!"

Neil plunged up the staircase, yelling, "You heard the lady!" and grabbed the man from behind.

He so surprised the attacker that the man released Annabeth's ankle. And the force Neil used sent him spinning back, half over the railing. Before Neil could get his hands on the bastard, the man did a balletic roll over the banister, dropped down from the staircase and beat a hasty retreat down the alleyway, crashing into what sounded like a resin garbage can.

Torn between going after him and seeing to Annabeth, who sat on a stair shaking, Neil stayed put.

When he helped her to her feet, she threw her arms around his neck tight enough to strangle him. He could feel the quick beat of her heart against his own. His body roused to the pulsing, and he wanted in the worst way to do something about it, but he figured she was vulnerable and he would be taking advantage. So he merely held on to her until she calmed down and pulled back.

Looking into her flushed face, he realized something different limned her expression than had earlier.

"Are you all right?"

"Am I all right?" she echoed, sounding more angry than scared. "That seems to be the question of the decade!"

Annabeth tested her limbs—all functional, Neil noted—but didn't give him a concrete answer. Then she leaned over and felt along a step until her fingers connected with something that jingled. When she straightened, her key ring was in hand. Suddenly, she focused on him, making him feel as if she'd forgotten he was there for a moment.

"You're welcome," he muttered.

"All right. Thank you. Again." She turned and went up the last few stairs to her door. In the midst of unlocking it, she turned back to him. This time her tone shifted to appreciative when she said, "That sounded ungrateful and I'm not, really, Neil. Thank you." She popped the front door open. "What are you doing here anyway?"

Hands on hips, he dryly said, "I thought I would take a midnight stroll in a strange neighborhood."

Annabeth sighed at his sarcasm. "Come on in."

Neil followed her across the threshold and was immediately enveloped by the warmth of the sparsely furnished place. A soft gold color washed the walls.

"Make yourself at home."

Neil sat on the couch backed with fluffy pillows in a rainbow of colors. He assumed Annabeth turned this into her bed at night...

To get his mind from such distractions, he said, "We need to call the police and make another report."

Now that she had calmed down, her face was pale and strained, washed out against her wheat-colored hair. Her normally soft-looking body seemed rigid and her hands curled into fists at her sides.

"I don't want to call the police just yet. Maybe not at all. It seems to be a waste of time, doesn't it? In any event, we need to talk about this first. And I need some tea." She dropped her keys on the table on the way into the kitchen. "What about you?"

Some instinct told Neil that he needed *her*—to take her in his arms and reassure himself that she was, indeed, okay. The legacy at work, he assured himself. But for now the tea would have to do.

"Tea sounds good," he said.

The apartment was so small that he could see her fill two mugs with water and set them in the microwave.

He went on. "The man who attacked you—"

"Nickels."

"You saw his face again?"

"I didn't have to. First the hostage situation, then my wallet being lifted and now this." Opening a canister and pulling out two tea bags, she said, "Obviously his intent at the rodeo was to get identification so that he could lie in wait for me and kill me without witnesses."

Neil feared that she had a point. "Maybe we should call Detective Wexler and go over everything with him personally. See if he agrees that all three incidents are related."

She poked her head out the kitchen door. "I was thinking that might be more productive than calling 911 again. At least he's spoken to us personally before."

The microwave dinged and she pulled out the mugs of hot water and dunked a tea bag in each. She asked how he liked his tea—plain—then joined him in the main room and handed him one of the mugs. She sat next to him, kicked off her shoes and curled her legs up on the couch behind her.

He couldn't help watching her. She held the mug with two hands. Her lashes fluttered closed as she took a long, slow sip. His pulse jumped at her small murmur of approval. She was close, disturbingly so. He almost got up and moved to the nearby chair. Then, again, no harm in enjoying a little closeness, he decided. A harmless activity.

Suddenly, she said, "I've come to a decision."

"About what?"

"About me. I have to fight back, Neil."

"So I noticed."

"Not just physically. Mentally." Her voice was a little shaky when she added, "I'll just disappear for good if I don't. I guess I haven't been myself for too long."

"Which is understandable. You just lost your brother."

"I lost myself a long time ago. I've been letting life swallow me whole. No more."

"Good. That's good."

"That's why I'm going to find Nickels."

"That's *not* good."

"And I need your help," she went on quickly before he could reason with her. Her blue eyes were wide. Vulnerable. "If you say no...well, I hope you won't say no. These visions of yours...you must be getting them for a purpose."

"To keep you out of danger."

"And the best way to do that," she said logically, "is to put Nickels behind bars."

"Leave it to the authorities, Annabeth."

"I can't. And neither can you," she insisted. "You can't tell them that you knew what was going to happen beforehand. They won't believe you. I'm a believer, though, whether or not I want to be."

Neil didn't like this. Not one bit. Annabeth was reminding him too much of his sister Kate, an earlier victim of the legacy. Kate had gotten so involved in a murder case—which was originally thought to be an accidental death—that she'd almost gotten herself killed.

He didn't want to see that happen to yet another woman he cared about.

Cared about?

"So what's your plan?" he asked stiffly. He had to know, had to at least pretend to cooperate if he was going to talk some sense into her. "I can't program myself to see things."

"How do you know? Have you ever tried?"

"I've never even had any kind of precognition before I met you."

Which brought him back to her certainty that he'd gotten the visions for a reason, which brought him full circle to his grandmother's legacy and her behest to put himself out in another's behalf.

Damn!

Maybe this was what he was supposed to do, Neil realized. Help her find Nickels. The reason he'd suddenly discovered his gift on his thirty-third birthday.

Fate…could he really fight it and win?

"All right," Neil conceded, "your point is a good one."

He could cooperate and protect Annabeth, make certain that she didn't run wild and end up facing death like Kate had. If he were more intimately involved, he could control the situation, Neil decided. Whenever he thought things were getting too dangerous, he could rein in Annabeth.

"But the only time I get this precognitive inspiration is when we're together," he continued. "So we need to be together more."

"That makes sense."

Neil knew Annabeth wasn't going to be thrilled

with his solution, but he kept his voice neutral, as if it didn't affect him in the least, when he said, "So you agree—I'll move my things in here tomorrow."

"You'll *what?*"

"You want my help, then we need to be together," he said logically.

"This place isn't big enough for the two of us."

Knowing she must be thinking of the sleeping arrangements, he said, "I've bunked down on hard ground more times than I care to count." And before she could come up with some other objection, he added, "Besides, if I get more involved, I'll be in as much danger as you are. I can't chance bringing that down on Skelly or Roz or three little kids."

Little kids who were in their terrible twos—which meant that chaos reigned in that particular McKenna household. Moving in with Annabeth would be peaceful by comparison.

But in order for the authorities to have the edge and round up Nickels and his cohort, Wexler needed to know everything that they did.

Except for the precognition thing, of course.

"Besides," Neil added, hoping this would be the clincher, "I intend to help you out with the rent. A man has his pride."

Annabeth stiffened but he could tell she was contemplating his offer. He could tell she didn't like it, but she didn't outright object, so he figured she was actually thinking about it.

And then suddenly she asked, "So you'll move in tomorrow?"

Her way of agreeing without saying the words?

Neil noticed her voice had been as purposefully neutral as his.

"Right. Tomorrow. But I don't plan on leaving you alone tonight."

She gulped hard. "Oh."

Not that she had anything to worry about from him. He could keep himself in check.

No matter how attractive he found her, he would feel honor-bound in her behalf to remain a gentleman, no matter how tempted he was to do otherwise.

ONLY AFTER TRYING to reach Detective Wexler, who proved unavailable until morning, did Annabeth fully consider the ramifications of taking in Neil as a roommate. At the moment, she was desperate for cash to pay her rent, but could she really take money from Neil? she wondered.

Having her rent paid would ease her mind a bit. And eventually—maybe sooner than later if Lloyd cut another check—she would repay Neil.

A woman had her pride, as well.

He was, after all, agreeing to something even more significant in helping her find Nickels. The idea that somehow, by some bizarre gift, he could ferret out the thief's lair, shook her. And if they did find him, what then?

And how were they to proceed?

Neil would have to touch her.

Maybe a lot.

Who knew how long it would take—how much touching—before they would get any results.

Annabeth grew warm just thinking about it. She

hadn't forgotten the kiss, certainly. No matter that she'd told herself to forget, that Neil wasn't for her. She didn't need further complications in her life—it was already more complicated than she'd ever imagined it could be. She didn't need a man. Didn't need anyone. Except maybe to help her out of this jam.

She'd give Neil that. She couldn't do it without him. Alone, where would she even start?

Realizing that she'd been in the bathroom for more than fifteen minutes, Annabeth figured that she had delayed the inevitable long enough.

After flushing the toilet and running the sink water for a moment to cover her retreat to calm her nerves, she threw open the door. Neil had slid down on the couch, had propped his boots on the table and had pulled his brimmed hat low on his forehead.

Had he fallen asleep? she wondered.

Tempted to leave him be, to delay the inevitable even more, to curl up in her chair and try to fall asleep, Annabeth knew she was being a coward. Before she could find her courage, he stirred. As if he could sense her staring at him, he flicked back the hat, straightened and turned to meet her gaze.

"Sorry," he muttered, his eyes slitted. "Guess I'm a little tired. You don't get to sleep in much when the household has three little kids."

"I guess not." Acting as if she didn't have a hesitation, Annabeth left the doorway. "I would be surprised if you weren't exhausted."

She eyed him warily as she took a seat at the other end of the couch, leaving a division between them.

He was staring at her openly now, and she imagined that his wolf's eyes nearly gleamed with yellow light.

"So how do we begin?" she choked out.

"By following our instincts. We could start by holding hands."

Great. Her palms were sweating. But when he slid closer and held out one of his, she hesitated only a second before giving over.

The first touch was electric and she started to pull her hand away, but he caught it and held fast.

Annabeth's eyes widened and her pulse fluttered. He wasn't hurting her but she felt his power. It was almost as if he kept her still by the force of his will. His gaze bore into her, stirring all her secret places. Her breathing grew shallow and her mouth went dry. Still, he didn't let go—neither her hand or otherwise.

She waited what seemed like an interminable amount of time before choking out, "Anything?"

He shook his head. "Not yet."

"How much longer do you suggest we try?"

"I don't know. I told you this is new to me. Maybe we need to be closer."

Before she could object that they hadn't been closer the previous times, he slid next to her.

Annabeth didn't know what this was doing for him, but she was certainly experiencing quite a reaction.

Her heart skipped a beat and she couldn't think straight. Though inches still separated them—except for the hand-holding—she imagined the heat of his body was pressed into hers. Now it wasn't just her palms that were sweating. She felt moist between her breasts and a trickle of wetness followed the curve of her spine.

"How is this working?" she whispered.

"Oh, it's working."

"What do you see?"

"Your beautiful blue eyes."

A thrill shot through her and though she tried to shake it away, she was a bit breathless when she clarified. "I meant in the way of a vision."

He shook his head. "I reckon I have to move closer."

Without further warning, Neil inched toward her so that they were sitting hip to hip, knee to knee. He slid an arm around the back of the couch, around *her* back. His fingers trailed over her far shoulder and down her upper arm.

And suddenly Annabeth was melting inside, trying to hang on to the purpose of this experiment.

She tried to speak but no words would come. Her open mouth seemed to be an invitation, because Neil took it. Literally. He slanted his mouth over her own and softly plundered its warm, wet interior.

Torn between wanting to pull away and indignantly demanding to know if *that* did it for him and wanting to let the kiss take her where it would, she drifted along in a haze of growing awareness.

Of him. Of her own sex-deprived body. Of how much more touching they could do without their clothes on.

Somehow her breast was in his hand and it seemed that Neil was considering the weight and firmness of the flesh. Then he found her nipple, which grew long and hard between his fingertips.

The time for analysis, for planning, for smart remarks was over.

Driven by pure instinct, Annabeth responded by slipping her hand along the front of his jeans. He adjusted himself so that she could more fully touch him. Even through the thick denim material, she could feel him, hard and long, as ready for sex as she. A warm wetness pooled between her thighs and she squirmed, wanting his hand—*him*—there.

Imagining him driving himself deep into her and riding her as smoothly as he had his horse earlier, Annabeth moaned. The guttural sound started low in her throat and resonated to every square inch of her aroused body.

Neil groaned, too.

And then, amazingly, set her aside.

Her hand felt abandoned as it lifted from temptation and the buzz in her head lightened.

"We ought to get to bed," he said, standing suddenly.

More turned on than she'd ever been in her life, Annabeth hazily reviewed the sleeping arrangements. The fact that she had one lone sofa bed kept sticking in her mind. Neil had said that he'd bunked on the ground before, but she suspected that kiss, those intimate touches, had been prelude to a deeper assault on the senses.

But with the physical connection broken, so was the fever that had raged in her only a moment ago. What had she been thinking? Well, of course she hadn't been thinking, had merely been driven by hormones.

Knowing that letting Neil make love to her would be a mistake, Annabeth readied herself for an argument.

Rising also, she announced, "Um, I need my sleep."

"So do I."

Without so much as looking her way, he started flipping the cushions to the floor.

"*Sleep,*" she emphasized.

"Are you trying to tell me something?"

"That's *my* bed."

"Got that."

"Where do you intend to sleep?"

He froze before he could release the last of the cushions. "Where do you *want* me to sleep?"

They locked gazes and his wolf's eyes practically swallowed her whole. Again, her breathing grew ragged. Temptation flitted through her body, but her mind was her strongest organ, she decided.

She crossed her arms over her chest as though she could stop her breasts from tingling. "You said you'd slept on the ground before."

"Uh-huh."

"So pick a spot and stop doing that."

"Doing what?"

"Looking at me as if you could eat me."

One dark eyebrow raised fractionally. "Sounds tempting, Sunshine. Where do you want me to start?" Neil asked as he moved in on her again.

He kept coming until Annabeth slapped a hand in

the middle of his chest. Squeezing her thighs together, she choked out, "That's far enough."

"I thought I would sleep between you and the door."

"Pick a spot on the floor!"

"That's what I meant."

To her utter embarrassment, after he swung open her bed, Neil began arranging the cushions that he had, of course, thrown between her and the door.

On the floor.

Maybe advanced intimacy was more on her mind than it was on his. Heat flooded her, but this time it wasn't seductive heat but pure embarrassment.

"Um, a pillow," she muttered. "You need a pillow. And sheets."

Thankfully, Annabeth was able to hide her red face for a moment in the closet where she stored her few extra linens. But even touching the pillow and sheets that would cover Neil's body gave her a goosey feeling that she found hard to ignore.

So by the time they settled down, lights out and silence reigning, she was wondering if she shouldn't have handled things differently. It had been so long since she'd slept with a man that she was ripe for picking.

Had she been just a bit more seductive...

Listening to Neil's soft snore a few minutes later, part of her mourned the fact that he hadn't been tempted enough to take a bite.

Chapter Nine

Dawn crept into Annabeth's apartment far too soon for Neil. Yet at the first rays of sunlight that crossed his makeshift bed on the floor, he arose.

Aware of the woman sprawled across the sofa bed only a few inches away—so close that he could reach out and touch her if he let himself—he knew that wouldn't be wise.

Not for him. Nor for her.

Annabeth slept on, sheet covering all of her, including her nose. Her wheat-colored hair spread out across her sky-blue pillowcase, a color that he was certain matched her eyes. When they were open, that was. At the moment, her long golden-brown lashes seemed glued to her cheeks.

His groin heavy with unsated need, he stared at her for too long, remembering what had almost happened between them the night before. He had wanted her more than any woman he'd ever known. He still wanted her.

Wanted to hold her…to kiss her…to make love to her until she forgot about bad karma and hostage situations and vile men who attacked her under the cover of night.

But she wouldn't forget, he knew. The resolve Annabeth had discovered in herself was strong, and it would be unfair of him to take that from her. She'd lost too much already and now she feared losing herself for good.

Neil didn't have a clue as to what such self-doubt would be like. He'd always known who he was, where he was headed, what goals he needed to accomplish. He'd lived his whole life with purpose.

But Annabeth…as far as he could tell, she'd been spinning her wheels, looking for a foothold somewhere. In something. She needed something to believe in. Someone. Herself.

He couldn't take that from her.

He would just have to let Annabeth do what she had to, Neil realized. He couldn't stop her or he would break her, perhaps beyond repair.

But at the same time, he vowed to protect her, to see her safely through this period of self-discovery.

Until Nickels and his partner were caught.

And then he would be out of her life. Mission accomplished. His grandmother's charge satisfied.

But would he be?

Not wanting to answer that question, Neil decided a temporary retreat was in order.

Moving quietly so as not to wake Annabeth, he grabbed his boots and slipped into the bathroom where he splashed his face with cold water, then used his damp hands to slick down his hair. The shower tempted him, but it could wait. A complete inspection of the area outside couldn't.

It had come to him during the interminable time when he'd tried to fall asleep that Nickels may have left behind something they could use, some clue.

Having hunted since he was a boy, Neil was an expert tracker. Whatever might be there, Neil would find.

Boots on, he crept through the apartment and out the front door, careful not to wake Annabeth. Once outside, he scanned every inch of the staircase with an eagle eye. He especially covered the area where Nickels had gone over the railing and was eventually rewarded by finding a few ragged threads caught on a splinter. He worked them free and placed them in his shirt pocket.

Nothing else presented itself at the staircase, but Neil followed Nickels's route into the alley. He noted the resin trash can the thief had knocked into—the lid had flown and stuck halfway open. Neil closed it and kept on. A box on the ground had been kicked halfway into the alley, and a bit farther along, he'd crunched over bottles, leaving shards of broken glass.

From there on, Neil found no visible trace of the bandit, but instinct kept him going. He smelled the man's trail—not literally, of course, but instinctively. Nearing the end of the alley, however, he stopped. Far enough. Going farther would serve no purpose but to frustrate himself. Nickels had probably left a car there—or perhaps his partner had been waiting for him.

But as he turned back, something dark and soft

between the garbage containers seemed to jump out at him. He reached behind and pulled out a piece of formed knit material. Inspecting it closer, he noted the face holes—the ski mask Nickels had been wearing.

Wondering what Detective Wexler might make of it, Neil jogged back to Annabeth's place.

He found her awake, making coffee. She startled at his reappearance. He also found her quite alluring in a buttercup-yellow nightshirt and a pair of athletic socks bunched at her ankles. Her long legs were bare and kissed with a golden glow that appeared to be natural.

A sudden image of *him* kissing those legs—tasting her skin—stopped him cold.

"I thought you'd left."

"I was looking around outside."

Her eyes widened and her knuckles whitened on the coffee can in her hands. "You saw someone? Or heard him?"

Sensing her impending panic, he was quick to reassure her. "Not at all. I was doing some investigating on my own. I'm an early riser."

"And?"

"And I found this."

Without moving, she stared at the ski mask in his hand. Her nostrils flared and her unbound breasts strained against the nightshirt as if she was having trouble breathing.

"Where?"

"At the end of the alley. Nickels must have tossed it when he figured he was safe."

She set down the coffee can. Then, with a trembling hand, she reached out to take the ski mask from him. The moment their fingers touched, tangled in the knit material, Neil lost all sense of the present...

Darkness falls as he walks down a main city street where old buildings, attached one to the other, rise several stories on either side.

Stopping to light a cigarette, he is vaguely aware of the rumble overhead and the streets filled with more oversize vehicles than compact cars. At a newsstand on the corner where triangular-shaped buildings stand sentinel over a six-corner intersection, an old black man hawks his wares. He stares at the stacks of newspapers and racks of magazines, the black lettering nothing more meaningful than a jumble to him. Then he switches his gaze to the magazines with X-rated eye candy and grins appreciatively before moving on.

A handful of young men with pierced ears, nose and eyebrows pass. Young artist-types meander along the streets in their gaudy, trendy outfits. He sneers at them. Then stares at the breasts on one of the passing women—a small lump, maybe a nipple ring, presses through the thin material of her tube top.

His reaction is swift and intense.

His gaze narrows to her spandex-clad bottom as he turns to follow the action. As if aware of his stare, she glances over her shoulder and with engorged red lips, kisses the air in his direction. When he waggles his tongue at her, she giggles, flips her hair and says something to her friend. They both laugh and hurry down the street.

He snorts and adjusts himself. Takes a drag on his cigarette. A cloud of smoke puffs before his face as he turns back to his original direction and saunters on.

A moment later, he turns into a doorway and glances briefly through the window with its neon signage advertising beer and booze. As usual, the bar area is mostly empty. The action is in back, around the pool table.

"What are you seeing?" Annabeth asked.

…snapping Neil straight back to the present.

"Seeing?" he echoed, struggling through a cloud of confusion to find Annabeth staring at him, her forehead pulled into a frown.

"You were having one of your visions, right?"

He nodded.

"So what was happening to me this time?"

Slowly, he shook his head. "Not you. Nickels. I think."

Neil looked down at the ski mask now solely in his hand. The vision must have collapsed the moment Annabeth had let go of the knit material. And him.

"You saw Nickels?" she asked, her voice low and anxiety-ridden.

"No. Odder. I *was* him. I saw what he saw. Not like the other times. Keelin can do that." He said of his Irish cousin, "Only she sees through the eyes of those in trouble. And she does so in her dreams, not when she's awake."

He puzzled over this new twist.

"The ski mask must have changed things," Annabeth said. "We've never held on to the same object before. Let's try it again."

Neil held the mask out to her. Annabeth licked her lips and grabbed hold of the knit.

Nothing.

"Maybe we're doing something different," she muttered, her forehead furrowed.

"We were touching before."

Annabeth tossed the hair over her shoulder and reached out again, this time grasping his fingers as well as the knit material.

Nothing—at least not of the precognitive variety.

Still staring at the spot where her hair cleared her neck, Neil shifted uncomfortably and blinked. He almost dropped his gaze to her breasts but he curbed that dangerous impulse. One good look at the more intimate parts of her anatomy might be too much to bear.

"It's not happening, is it?"

"No vision, no."

Other things were happening though, no matter where he set his gaze.

Her neck…her mouth…her eyes…all were becoming dangerous territory.

Damn The McKenna Legacy—it was making a sex-crazed idiot of him. That and the vision. Nickels would be a horny bastard. Neil could still sense the man's reaction as he surveyed the luscious attributes of the young woman sauntering down the street.

Making a sound of frustration that he could relate to, Annabeth backed off and crossed her arms under her breasts, which only served to bring their size and perfect shape to his attention.

Remembering the feel of her nipple as it grew long and hard between his fingers, of the weight of a full, womanly breast, gave him an instant erection.

Clenching his jaw, Neil turned and looked away toward safer territory. "Listen, Annabeth, maybe you'd better try calling Detective Wexler again."

"What are you going to do?"

"Step in the, uh…other room for a minute, if you don't mind."

He thumbed toward the bathroom.

"Oh. No, of course not."

Annabeth went for the phone and Neil whipped into the bathroom, thankful for a moment's privacy.

What he'd like to do was take a cold shower. But he confined himself to washing his hands and spraying his wrists and face and neck with cold water.

Several times.

When he emerged a few minutes later, he was relieved to see Annabeth fully dressed in jeans and a loose shirt. The telephone receiver was at her ear.

"Detective Wexler? Annabeth Caldwell. I think we need to talk," she said, then paused for a moment. "No. In person." Another pause. "Your place or mine?"

It seemed Wexler wanted out of the office, for he agreed to meet them at Annabeth's apartment.

Now the problem was…how much should they tell him?

"YOU'RE SLIPPING, amigo."

His failure to shut down Annabeth Caldwell permanently already eating at him, he paced the broken-down space that served as a hideaway in the midst of a trendy neighborhood.

"Slipping, my ass." He stopped to glare at the Hispanic. "No way could I have predicted that she wouldn't be alone."

"He get a good look at you?"

"That's the one thing. My saving grace." With a feral grin, he informed the other man, "That ski mask of yours came in handy. Thanks."

The Hispanic man's face drained of color. "What you do with it?"

"What? You think you need it now, in the middle of summer? I'll buy you a new one."

"You got rid of it?"

"Damn straight."

"Where?"

"In the alley."

"Near *her* place? They got all this sophisticated testing now. You ever heard of DNA? They already got me before. You crazy—!"

He had the Hispanic by the throat before the man could finish, saying, "If I'm crazy, then you had best watch your back." For good measure—and just because he felt like it—he threw the smaller man against a wall. "Don't underestimate me, *pancho,* that would be a mistake."

He stared hard, but the Hispanic didn't flinch.

"Watching your back goes two ways, amigo..."

NEIL RODE EARLY. Though he roped his calf in an excellent time, he didn't stay to see if he had won the night's round.

Instead, he searched out Annabeth who was waiting for him on the sidelines.

Wexler had called back—a more important case was breaking and he promised to get to her as soon as he was free. Apparently not yet. Annabeth wasn't about to wait and Neil couldn't talk her out of it, so he conceded and they made plans of their own. They would start their own hunt for Nickels now, just before dark, just as it had been in the vision.

Perhaps if they found the neighborhood and the bar, they would find the thief.

To "disguise" themselves, they both wore baseball caps. Neil had also donned one of Skelly's Bulls T-shirts.

Annabeth already had her hair tucked up out of sight. That, added to a pair of lycra pants and a halter top, and she looked totally unlike herself.

But great, Neil thought.

Sexy.

Certainly not the wholesome farm girl he'd gotten used to.

Neil wasn't sure he liked her going out in public so blatantly sexual, especially considering the way Nickels had slobbered after the girl on the street. Annabeth was even more tempting, and Neil was having a difficult time getting his mind off the fact.

But he was her shadow, Neil reminded himself. He would see that no harm came to her.

He cleared his throat. "So you think this Bucktown-Wicker Park area is the one?"

They were cutting across the Loop, the business

office-shopping-theater district, ringed by the elevated
track that literally made a loop. All was comparatively
quiet now.

"It fits the description. Probably several neighbor-
hoods do to some extent," Annabeth admitted. "But
offhand, I can't think of another with six corners *and*
the elevated structure."

She guided him out of the Loop and onto Milwau-
kee Avenue, an angled street that led right into the
heart of the Bucktown-Wicker Park neighborhood.
Altogether, it was a mere fifteen-minute drive from
the rodeo grounds. As they approached the intersec-
tions at North and Damen—their destination—traffic
clogged the streets and slowed them to a crawl.

"I could get a horse through here easier than a
truck," he groused.

"Yeah, but how would the horse feel about it?"

Neil merely grunted.

At least the traffic gave him plenty of time to look
around. The people on the streets certainly could have
been the ones in his vision. But having to keep half
his mind on driving wasn't the best way to identify
anything. He would have to park his truck and they
would have to canvass the area on foot.

Parking was a seemingly impossible task in this
particular city, but he found a spot two blocks past
the main intersection. Of course it wasn't legal. But
if they *didn't* take it...

Neil parked.

"Kind of deserted out this way," Annabeth murmured as they left the truck.

Neil noted a couple of old manufacturing buildings and some new construction.

"Except for the vehicles, of course," he said. "Plenty of those."

Undoubtedly the drivers were all in the hot spots ahead—restaurants and clubs and coffeehouses. As they walked along the lonely street, Neil had plenty of time to take in his surroundings. A rapid-transit train sliced overhead even as they crossed under the elevated tracks.

Annabeth shivered.

"You're not cold?"

"Anticipation," she murmured.

He knew what she meant. His sense of certainty grew as they approached the six-corner intersection.

"That building." He pointed to the pale triangular shape across the street. "I recognize that one."

"The Flatiron Building."

Annabeth's knowing the structure's name probably meant it was some kind of landmark, Neil decided, his gaze settling on a small structure on the corner.

"There's the newsstand," he said with satisfaction. "This is it, then. We're on our way."

A sense of triumph filling him, Neil wrapped an arm around Annabeth's shoulders and led her across the street. Now if only everything else fell into place so smoothly.

"There's a bar ahead," she said.

He looked it over. "Nope. Too fancy. Look for an old-time place. Lots of neon advertisements filling the windows."

Neil hung on to Annabeth as they struggled through

the crowd gathering around a doorway from which blaring hip-hop issued.

As they waited to get into the club, most dressed in black and wearing platform shoes, body parts pierced and/or tattooed, hair spiked or braided and dyed bright colors, the young people chattered so loudly their voices competed with the so-called music.

Two doors down an elegantly dressed couple most likely in their late thirties exited a limo and headed for the door of a fancy restaurant.

Quite an eclectic neighborhood.

Suddenly, Annabeth grabbed onto his arm, asking, "Did the bar look something like that one?" She pointed him to an establishment farther down the block.

"Exactly like that one," he murmured, hurrying her along the crowded street.

A moment later, they were peering through the windows. Neil caught sight of a familiar-looking pool table in back. A couple of guys, wreathed in smoke, were playing.

"Ready?"

Annabeth nodded. "Let's go inside."

They'd found the neighborhood. They'd found the bar. Now if only three really were a charm, they would find Nickels, as well, and have him arrested.

Then he and Annabeth could relax.

Get back to their lives.

Separately.

As he swung open the door, Neil tried to ignore the twinge that last idea caused him.

CASUALLY, NEIL LED Annabeth past the bar toward the back. She kept her gaze covert rather than forthright, but she didn't miss a thing. Two guys and one lone woman sat at the bar. Several more people sat or stood around the pool table. No one she recognized.

None of them Nickels.

"I don't see him."

"That *would* be too easy," Neil said in a low voice. "You get a table over there and I'll get us something from the bar. Any preferences?"

"A beer would be fine. Lite."

While Neil ordered their drinks, she gazed around the room. Dark and a little seedy, the place was a throwback to the old neighborhood. PG—pregentrification. The patrons were throwbacks, too. People who hadn't yet been forced out by the high prices.

Only a matter of time, she thought, her mind wandering a bit to her family homestead that had been eaten up by a corporation. She wondered if she would even recognize the place now.

A fact that brought her good mood down a notch.

"Here you go."

Startled, she realized Neil had set down a beer right in front of her. And he was sliding into the chair with his back to the wall, undoubtedly so that he could see anyone who entered from the street.

She took a sip and asked, "You don't think Nickels could have been here and gone already?"

"It's just getting dark now."

She glanced toward the windows, dusky smudges

with pinpricks of light shining through as vehicles passed on the street.

"How long do you think we have to wait?" she asked.

"Can't say. No way for me to know if today is even the right day."

At least he was honest.

Sighing, Annabeth took a slug of beer. Her anticipation turned a bit sour. She had been hoping so much that she would nail Nickels, and this anxiety would be over...

Then she could get on to building a new life for herself.

The only drawback being that Neil would finish out the week and return to South Dakota, and she would never see him again.

A fact that saddened her more than it should have, she thought.

She gave him a sideways glance and wondered if he was thinking something similar himself. He was staring at her again. He seemed to do that a lot. Warmth crept through her, but she blamed it on the beer.

And yet she wanted to acknowledge the man. "Neil, thank you for agreeing to help me."

"You didn't leave me much choice."

"I didn't wrestle you to the ground to force you," she said with a laugh.

"I couldn't let you flounder around on your own. The legacy," he quickly added. "My grandmother Moira wouldn't have approved."

"Of me?"

"Of my abandoning you."

She widened her eyes. "Then you're saying she *would* have approved of me?"

"I think she would have approved of you just fine."

His mellow tone skittered along her skin, made the short hairs along her arms and down the back of her neck stand to attention.

"What about you?" she asked, a tad too breathless. "I mean, I know you're attracted to me, but that's just physical."

"That makes me sound shallow." Which made him sound a bit indignant. He leaned in toward her. "I'm attracted to more than the way you look."

The breath caught in her throat. "As in?"

"As in your soft heart."

"There's no way for you to know that."

"Of course there is. You've told me about your family, remember. I hear your heart in your voice when you speak of them."

She knew family was important to Neil. What she didn't know was why his responses were so important to her.

His smile was crooked when he looked away from her at the back room where a pool game was in session.

Annabeth allowed her gaze to wander to the bar and one of the guys now parked there. He hadn't been there before, she was certain.

Something about him made her stare.

His broad back to them, he was sitting alone. His

dark hair was slicked back, his skin naturally tanned. But his head was lowered, his face turned away.

Still, something about him...

When her gaze wandered to his forearm as he picked up his beer to take a swig, and his rolled sleeve slipped to reveal a bit more of his arm, she nearly choked on her own beer.

Annabeth poked Neil to get his attention.

"The guy at the bar," she said in a low voice, indicating the loner with a furtive nod.

"Nickels?" he asked doubtfully.

She shook her head. "His partner. Look at the tattoo on his forearm."

The man raised his drink one last time and emptied it. The rolled sleeve slipped all the way back.

"A skull."

"With a rose in its teeth," she whispered. "I saw that rose on the Hispanic thief."

"You're sure it's the same one?"

"That would be some coincidence if it wasn't."

The man set down his mug and pushed away from the bar, turning in his stool so they got a good look at his mustachioed face. Then he got to his feet and stretched as if he was ready to leave.

"So what do we do now?" Annabeth mumbled into the beer she picked up to cover her face. Through lowered lashes, she was watching him move toward the exit.

Neil said, "I think we follow him."

Chapter Ten

Determined not to lose the thief now that they'd spotted him, Neil hung onto Annabeth's hand as they dodged a handful of pedestrians. The chase along the darkened street seemed a bit unreal. Then so did everything that had happened so far, he decided.

"He's going so fast," Annabeth gasped out. "You don't think he saw us?"

"Not yet."

"What if he does?"

"We'll have to get creative to put him off the scent."

The light at the intersection ahead changed, forcing the thief to stop at the curb. Neil stopped also, right where he was, and whipped Annabeth into the side of the Flatiron Building so that he could shelter her from view with his body.

"This is what you call creative?" she asked, her voice tight.

"It's the best I could come up with on short notice." Figuring she could see over his shoulder, he said, "Let me know when the light turns green again.

And don't be too obvious, but tell me if Tattoo-man looks our way.''

"Tattoo-man?" she echoed.

"Okay, Skull-man."

With no better way of identifying him, Neil thought to dub the nameless thief for his tattoo.

"Skull-man...Skull."

"Skull it is," Neil agreed.

Crossing at a six-corner intersection was an exercise in patience, considering the extra set of lights and all, so he knew they would remain standing there, pressed close together for several minutes.

Long enough to make Neil shift uncomfortably.

Long enough for Annabeth to notice.

The streetlight shone in her eyes that had gone all big on him. As if realizing that she was revealing something she would rather keep from him, Annabeth immediately shifted her gaze back over his shoulder.

Even so, Neil could tell that she was still as distracted as he. The attraction that had been building between them seemed to be approaching the speed of light.

All he had to do was touch her...look at her...think of her...to be turned on.

Purposely putting a slight gap between their bodies as if that might help cool things down, he said, "Warn me about that light."

At which time they would smoothly pull away from the building and back into tracking Skull. They'd have to time this perfectly so that they didn't catch up to the Hispanic, while still managing to get across the street on the same light as he did.

If they missed their shot, they would lose him.

"There," she gasped. "Now!"

Thankful to put a little space between them, Neil caught Annabeth's wrist and headed for the intersection at a near trot. They had to go around a group of artsy-looking types who stopped at the intersection arguing and blocking foot traffic. He could see that Skull had already crossed the first street and was setting foot into the second.

Neil put on some speed to play catch-up. He and Annabeth were only halfway across the second street when the light changed and an impatient driver leaned on his horn.

The blare cut though the night and caught the thief's attention. He glanced back, and for one heart-stopping moment, Neil thought Skull recognized them...until he merely turned away and continued strolling up the street.

"That was close."

"Where do you think he's headed?"

"Either a parked vehicle or some nearby destination."

"Should we take the truck?"

Neil considered the option for a moment, long enough for Skull to cross the street in the middle of the block and cut toward a vacant lot.

"No truck."

Now it would get tricky, Neil thought. They would be in the open. If Skull glanced back when they were following him, he would know.

"If he sees us together again, he'll get suspicious," Annabeth muttered, as if she could read his mind.

"Maybe we should split up and stay on two sides of him. I can go this way and you can—"

"Forget it."

"But he might see us, figure out what's going on."

"We'll have to take that chance."

"We're already taking a chance," she argued.

But Neil wasn't letting Annabeth out of his sight. He shuddered to think of what Skull would do to her should he catch her alone.

"We're staying together."

"I have something to say in this."

"No, you don't, not this time."

"But—"

"No buts. C'mon."

Once again, Annabeth was reminding Neil of his sister. The risk-taking part that made him crazy. Annabeth was willing to go too far. Even together, they weren't really safe.

What if Skull was leading them straight to Nickels? Which would be good if he didn't know he was being followed. But what if the thief did? He could be stringing them along, leading them into a trap.

A trap set by two dangerous men, no doubt both armed. And this time, with a single focus. No cops, no negotiators, just *them*.

How would he protect Annabeth then? Neil wondered, with the odds so bad. How had he gotten himself into such a mess?

He tried talking himself out of the speculation as they followed Skull's shortcut under the elevated tracks. When a train rumbled overhead, Neil hurried, but he wasn't fast enough. They were assaulted by grit sifting down on them as the train squealed along.

"Great," Annabeth muttered, brushing loose particles from her hair and clothing.

"Don't worry about it," Neil whispered. "Distractions could get us killed."

He looked around them. Only dark and more dark, he thought, hurrying to keep up.

Suddenly Annabeth tripped over something Neil couldn't see. "Easy," he whispered as he stopped her from falling.

She must have made a noise loud enough to catch Skull's attention, for he suddenly turned back. Neil caught Annabeth in his arms and pressed her into the cold dirty elevated structure as if for a tryst.

To make it realistic, he kissed her.

Not a quick, light touch of the lips, but a full-bodied assault. His body against hers was feeling more and more familiar, more and more seductive.

More and more frustrating.

When he came up for air, Neil wondered how much more torture he could take.

AGITATED BY her wholehearted response to Neil, Annabeth wondered what in the world she had been thinking.

Nothing, of course. She hadn't been thinking at all. She'd been responding.

Mindlessly.

"I think it's safe now, don't you?" she gasped out in a low voice.

"Yeah, probably."

''Then you can get off me.''

''Oh. Right.''

Neil pushed himself away, allowing her to breathe. Trying to ignore her hormones and to settle down, Annabeth looked around him.

''Damn, he's gone!''

She pushed by Neil and crossed the expanse of open lot as fast as she could, knowing he was right at her side. He tried to take her hand, but she avoided him. She was tired of being pushed and led and bullied into doing things his way as if she were a child.

They hit the side street in the midst of an old manufacturing district surrounded by bungalows and two flats. Frantically, she peered into the dark for any shape that she could identify as belonging to Skull and panicked for a moment until she saw something moving near one of the old, boarded-up factory buildings.

She pointed. ''There.''

Sweet relief filled her. She would never have forgiven herself if they'd lost him.

''That building looks deserted.''

Figuring Neil meant *dangerous,* Annabeth started for it before he could stop her. ''Good for someone on the run, I guess.''

''You're not going to follow him in there.''

''You have a better idea?''

He grabbed her arm and jerked her to a stop. ''Yes, I can stake him out and you can go find a phone and call Wexler. Get reinforcements.''

''And leave you alone? I think not.''

''I can take care of myself.''

"Well, so can I." A blatant untruth in this particular situation, but Annabeth's ire was up. "Besides, Wexler isn't sitting by a phone, waiting for my call." By the time she got help, Neil could be...

Neil pulled her closer to the corner bungalow where they stood in the dark. The front porch was lit up, but the interior lights were out, as if no one was home.

"What's wrong with you? Are you *trying* to get yourself killed? Is that your solution to ending your misery?"

Annabeth gaped. "Who the hell do you think you are, talking to me that way?"

"The man who saved your pretty little behind. More than once, I might add. And maybe the only person in this city who cares what happens to you."

Her anger deflating like a flat tire, Annabeth felt a prickle at the backs of her eyes. "Y-you care?"

"Why the hell else would I be going through all of this?" he asked indignantly. "Not because I think it's fun. I'm doing it *for you.* So that you can sleep at night. So that you can believe you're alive. *Really* alive."

Tears sprang to her eyes. Trying to maintain a tough facade was impossible in the face of his confession. Suddenly, she felt a lot less alone. No one had been around to tell her they cared since her mother had left the city.

Big, fat, embarrassing tears clung to her lashes and threatened to choke her. Using the back of her hand, she dashed them away and mumbled, "Okay, then."

"Okay?"

Hearing the suspicion in his tone, she added, "Yeah."

Annabeth wanted to fist his silly Bulls T-shirt and pull him toward her so that she could kiss him again. Properly. But now was not the time or place. Now could very well get them killed. She had to keep that in mind...

"So...do you know how to drive a truck?" he asked.

"I was raised on a farm. Of course. But what does that have to do with anything?"

"If Skull leaves here in a vehicle and we decide to follow, we can't because we're on foot. I thought you might consider going back and getting my truck, bringing it down that side street."

Neil was sounding way too reasonable, Annabeth decided. *Consider?* Where had that come from?

"I thought you were insisting that I stay glued to your side."

"I didn't want you facing a criminal alone, Annabeth. It wasn't meant as any kind of insult to you. I don't want to see you get hurt. Maybe worse."

Maybe worse. Yeah, *worse* was a big word in her vocabulary these days.

"You're not just trying to get rid of me so that you can go in there alone and be some kind of macho hero?

"I don't have a single hero-gene in my body," he promised.

"Liar," she said softly. "I never met a real live hero until you, Neil Farrell. Okay, give me your keys."

He dug in a pocket and handed them over to her. "Be careful."

"Back at you. I won't be long."

Even as she retraced their path at a jog, Annabeth knew the potential for violence lay behind her. She suspected Neil knew that, as well, and wanted her out of danger's path.

Well, not for long. She wasn't going to let him take all the risk.

Glancing back to make certain he was still there, Annabeth didn't see him. The breath caught in her throat and she screeched to a halt. Then she caught sight of a male silhouette near the bungalow porch that told her that he was just playing cautious. She was able to breathe again.

Setting off anew, she was thankful that he wasn't advancing on the place alone.

Maybe she should call for reinforcements. But where to do so? The truck wasn't exactly parked in a hot spot where she could just waltz into a restaurant or bar and demand they call 911.

She would have to drive somewhere. Park again. Waste a lot of time. Perhaps crucial time. Time enough that Skull could get away.

Or Neil could get hurt.

Nope, she would stick to the latest plan, just plain bring Neil's truck around the way he'd asked.

Crossing under the elevated structure, Annabeth felt more positive than she had in a long time. Having coerced Neil into helping her, she'd viewed finding the thieves as an uphill battle. But now it seemed that he *wanted* to help her. She could count on him to partner her, to see her through this.

Not that she hadn't already known that on some level.

Neil was truly a man of honor and courage—he would do whatever he could to help her. And then he would return to his own life.

And once more she would be alone.

The truck was in sight and so was the orange ticket attached to the driver's window and flapping in the breeze.

"Damn!"

Trying to decide whether to rip the thing up or just throw it in the glove compartment for now and tell him about it later, she chose the second option.

Carrying out that plan, Annabeth refused to let the knowledge that Neil would soon be gone bring her down. She would live for now. For the moment. And when Neil left, she would be happy for him. Happy that he had a place and a life that he loved and to which he could return.

Only…she didn't want to face this part…she'd known him for such a short time…a part of her heart would go with him.

"I DON'T KNOW how much longer I can stay awake," Annabeth said with a yawn. "Maybe we ought to leave and call the police, after all."

"Not yet. Not when we're this close. If you're tired, give in to it, get some rest."

"Then how will you stay awake?"

"I'll manage."

After midnight and no sign of life. Chances were, there wouldn't be, Neil knew. Chances were, Skull was asleep...

Skull. Neil was certain that his vision had played out through the Hispanic's eyes.

He couldn't figure it unless...the ski mask belonged to Skull and not Nickels.

But why would the Hispanic be after Annabeth? She hadn't seen his face. Which made Neil wonder how much influence Nickels had over his cohort. Either that, or the thief was just plain paranoid or angry because she'd gotten so close to escaping, and he wanted to get even.

Annabeth's head against his shoulder had grown heavier, her breathing softer. And Neil was torn between putting an arm around her to hold her closer...or leaving her in the safety of his truck while he went to investigate the old factory building.

Not that he was trying to be heroic.

He merely wanted some result from their night's investigation. Maybe leaving and calling the police in again would be the wisest move. But it had to be Wexler. And Wexler had proven to be unavailable.

Neil didn't have long to dwell on the question, for Annabeth began making small noises in her sleep. Small scared noises. He wrapped that arm around her and pulled her close. But though he tried to soothe her with his touch, she resisted and thrashed and cried out.

"Sunshine," he called softly. "Wake up. You're dreaming."

With a great suck-in of air, she awoke, eyes wide,

body shaking. Her fear was palpable and he could feel her pulse beneath his palms.

"Neil…"

She breathed <u>his name</u> and the soft sound stirred the short hairs at the back of his neck.

"Shh, it's all right now," he assured her as he had in his vision. This is what he'd seen the night he had first kissed her. "It was only a dream."

"No, he knows where I am…he can get to me at any time…"

"But I'm here with you," he said soothingly. "You're not alone."

"Not alone," she echoed.

Her wide-open blue eyes swam with unwept emotion.

Then she touched him, her fingers fluttering to the side of his face. He sighed and turned his head so that his lips touched her fingers, then her open palm.

"Neil…"

"Annabeth…"

His mouth was barely centimeters from hers.

She turned in his arms so that her body was against his. Her fear beat against him as her heart drummed a message to his. They were breasts to chest, hip to hip, lips to lips.

Her fear became his. He was lost for a moment, until terror turned to raging desire…

Neil couldn't help himself. He couldn't stop from kissing her any more than a starving man could stop himself from eating when a buffet was spread before him. Annabeth was the most tempting, irritating, lovely, frustrating woman he'd ever held in his arms.

And it seemed Annabeth was as starving as he, for she kissed him with fervor and explored him through his clothing. Her light touch spread fire as she trailed her fingers down the length of his neck to his chest to his waist. Then she snaked her hand along his belt and around to the back, where she tucked her fingertips below his waistband.

Neil groaned and shifted as his groin throbbed.

And he returned the favor, starting at the small of her back and ending by cupping her breast.

"Neil…" she breathed into his mouth. "Yes…"

Suddenly a shot of hazy light issued from the darkened factory building. Neil stopped the kiss just as the front door was opening.

"Annabeth," he said, "look."

The light was off now, but the streetlights were enough to see Skull leaving the building and pulling the door shut behind him.

"Where do you think he's going?" Annabeth murmured as she squirmed away, setting a good distance between them. "Could he be meeting up with Nickels?"

She was breathless but trying to sound normal, Neil thought. Surely she wasn't embarrassed. Now was not the time to talk things over, however.

For the Hispanic thief was unlocking an ancient Monte Carlo. He opened the driver's door and slid in behind the wheel.

Getting hold of himself, Neil said, "My question is whether or not to follow him."

"Why wouldn't we? I thought that's why I got the truck."

As the thief started his engine, Neil admitted, "I'm curious about what we might gain by getting inside the building."

"You mean as in *break in?*"

"I wouldn't put it like that. Not exactly. Besides, the place is an old, deserted factory, not an apartment building. Who says the bastard was in there legally?"

Rationalizing had never been Neil's forte, but it seemed he was getting good at lots of things he'd never done before. Besides, his logic really did make sense to him. If they left the place now, and waited for the police to go in, any evidence could disappear.

The Monte Carlo started pulling away from the curb...

"Well, go or stay?" he asked Annabeth.

She hesitated only a moment before saying, "Stay. Let's see where he's been holing up."

Thankfully, she was sounding normal. The fear she'd awakened with had dissipated along with the sexual tension that had hot-wired between them only moments ago.

Neil felt under his seat for his flashlight. The moment the old car turned a corner, they were out of the truck and heading for the darkened building.

"So how will we get in?" Annabeth asked.

"Windows are pretty low."

"That doesn't mean they're open."

"In the kind of heat we've been having?"

Not that they had to make the effort. The front door was unlocked. After circling the entire building to make certain he spotted no other sign of life through the darkened windows, Neil shone his light on the door and found the locks had been jimmied open.

"Our friend Skull must not have a key," Neil murmured. "Stay here a moment."

"Why?"

"In case he comes back," Neil lied.

He intended to double-check the interior, to make certain they were alone. Nickels could be in there. Asleep. Waiting. A spider in his web. Neil wouldn't subject Annabeth to any more danger than necessary.

Without fully opening the door, he slipped inside and quietly moved through an entry area and toward a cavernous space that had once been the factory.

Moonlight filtered in through the filthy windows and illuminated the interior. Empty. Almost. All the machines that had once kept this factory humming were long gone. Everything that could be stripped from the interior was gone.

Neil stood in the shadows, listening, until his eyes adjusted and he could sweep the interior more efficiently. No sign of life. No sound.

Even so, he clicked on his flashlight and shone it around to be certain. The beam caught the "living area"—an old couch, a small table and two chairs and a single bed. All vacant. Weird. How could someone be living here? Unless it was for the guard. But there didn't seem to be a guard...

A chill shot through Neil as he wondered what might have happened to the fellow.

Returning to the entry, he softly called out, "Annabeth, c'mon in."

He found a bank of light switches. A few dim bulbs went on, casting the interior with menacing shadows.

"I didn't see anyone on the street," she volunteered.

"Good. Let's go through this place quickly before anyone is the wiser."

Not much to go through at that. Girlie magazines on the floor near the bed. A few clothes hung up on a pole. Of course, it was too much to hope that any of the cowboy duds from the robbery would be there.

Annabeth was digging through a garbage can filled with fast-food wrappings. "Yuk!" she muttered. "Doesn't this guy ever eat anything that isn't greasy?"

More trash littered the table and floor. Neil moved some of it around with his boot until he hit an odd lump. He kicked away the bag covering it and revealed something small and dark and square.

"What's this?" he muttered, stooping to pick up what proved to be a worn leather wallet.

"Oh, my God," Annabeth whispered.

"Is this what I think it is?"

She nodded. "Proof." And then, voice hopeful, she said, "Maybe my check is still inside."

Holding the thing gingerly so as not to mess any telling prints, Neil held it out to her. "You do the honors."

Annabeth's hand trembled as she reached out to take the wallet from him. Her fingertips touched his and Neil's mind whirled into the mist...

"La-a-adies and gentlemen. May I direct your attention to the bucking chute."

Audience laughter fills the arena as the chute opens and a docile horse steps out, a rodeo clown on his back facing the wrong direction. Despite the fact, he pumps his legs and throws up his free arm as if he's riding a bronc.

The view shifts closer, behind the scenes, to a pen where calves rounded up for the next event are being held.

Nearby, a cowboy flips a coin over and over as he gazes around from beneath the brim of his hat. Stuffing the coin into his vest pocket, he reaches behind him and surreptitiously pulls out a knife.

Emotions crash, one upon the other. Animosity...fear...hatred...resentment...the need for revenge. Some flow from him like a river of destruction, but an equally strong force meets and counters them...

The cowboy turns his head toward an unsuspecting Annabeth, who is getting ready to work the chute.

Watching her, he caresses the wicked blade...

Chapter Eleven

"Neil."

Annabeth called his name softly several times before acknowledgment entered his gaze.

Aware that he'd seen something upon touching her wallet, she thought to give him a minute to come back to earth. Neil shook his head as if to clear it, then swore under his breath.

Pulse ticking too fast, she asked, "You saw through Skull's eyes again?"

"No," Neil said slowly. "I saw someone else. Nickels, I think."

Her stomach twisted. "You saw him? You weren't seeing through his eyes like last time?"

Neil shook his head. "Someone else's. Someone watching him watch…" Letting his words drift off, he frowned and looked away. "It was…confusing."

"How so?"

"I was tapping into emotions. Strong ones. Only they weren't all his."

"There *are* two of them," she reminded him while handling the wallet carefully so as not to screw up any telltale fingerprints. Mentally crossing her fingers and toes that her check was still tucked away inside, she opened it. "Maybe you somehow tapped into both Nickels and Skull."

"Right. It just felt…different somehow. I can't explain it. Sorry."

Empty.

The check was gone along with all of her cash.

Annabeth sighed. "Yeah, me, too." Without touching any more of the leather than she had to, she dropped the wallet into her pocket. "What do you say we get out of here?"

"Fine by me."

Neil was suddenly acting odd, distracted, scaring her. And Annabeth was too chicken to ask him what was wrong. So as they made their cautious way back to the truck, a fine wire of tension hung between them.

Suddenly Neil said, "Do me a personal favor and don't report for work tomorrow."

Personal? Annabeth's heart picked up a beat. There was that caring side of him again. Too bad she couldn't agree. "You know I have to go."

"Which is more important—money or your life?"

Her life? Which meant what exactly?

As Neil opened the passenger door for her, Annabeth stalled getting inside. First things first. Knowledge was power, but she was feeling very little of that at the moment.

"What did you leave out, Neil? What are you trying *not* to tell me?"

For a moment, she thought he wasn't going to answer, then, sounding stiff, he admitted, "Nickels was at the rodeo. He was watching you work, watching your every move.''

Now he really had her spooked. The hair at the back of her neck was prickling and she was finding it difficult to swallow. But she wasn't about to cave.

"I have no choice, Neil."

"So you're saying the money is more important."

"No, it goes beyond the monetary. I'm not willing to let a criminal dictate what I do with my life." And there was more. Even the thought set her stomach flip-flopping and tying itself into a knot. "Besides which, it's a perfect opportunity to catch the bastard, isn't it?"

"Annabeth, what are you thinking? You're intending to put yourself out as bait?"

That Neil sounded shocked didn't surprise her. If she was normally levelheaded, then he was downright cautious, overly cautious, even for her. She'd never met a man who could be so uptight.

"Why not?" she asked.

"Because it's too damn dangerous!"

"It's *my* life. My decision."

"Lord, when you're reckless and stubborn like this, you do remind me of Kate!"

"Leave your sister out of this."

"Why? She put herself into situations…" With a sound of frustration, he lapsed into a silence thick with unspoken censure.

So he cared about her? Like Kate? Annabeth wondered. *Like a sister?*

Her voice thickening in her throat, she muttered, "What can Nickels do to me in a crowded arena?"

"Who says that's where he'll come after you?"

"I'm not going to go off by myself again."

The streetlight illuminating his torn expression, Neil stared down at her, and Annabeth knew there was more.

Finally, he said, "Nickels had a knife."

Imagining the cold-eyed bastard watching her, with a sharp blade made her swallow hard. "Then we'll have to be doubly careful that he doesn't get to me."

"It's a foolhardy plan."

"Desperate, maybe, but not foolhardy."

"Following someone in the open is one thing," he said, "but using you as bait...we're amateurs, for God's sake!"

"Then we'll just have to get help from the authorities."

"PRECOGNITION, huh?" Sitting on the couch with Annabeth early the next morning, his partner in the chair opposite, Detective Wexler seemed to be biting back a grin.

"You do readings on the side, Farrell?" Detective Smith asked.

Annabeth winced. Their amusement was not a good sign.

She gave Neil an *I told you so* expression. Saying they had no other way of explaining how they'd known where to find the Hispanic thief, he'd made the decision to reveal all, including his visions.

"Your sarcasm isn't appreciated, Wexler," Neil said.

The detective immediately sobered. "Neither is your screwing me around."

"All right, believe what you will." Annabeth quickly interceded before they lost Wexler altogether. "The fact is that I was attacked. Twice in one night. And then we found the damn wallet after following a man with a tattoo like that on one of the thieves who got away. Kind of a coincidence, huh, especially considering I'm the only one who saw Nickels's face the day before."

They'd already handed over the wallet and ski mask in plastic bags. They'd told him about her wallet being stolen and their theory that Nickels had been the culprit so that he could get her address. They'd also given him the location of the factory building.

Wexler nodded. "Sorry for the skepticism. You can hardly blame us. But about the attacks...I believe you're right. This Nickels character undoubtedly seems responsible for both incidents."

Annabeth was relieved that Wexler was taking them seriously in general if not in the particulars.

"So what do you plan to do about it?" Neil asked.

Wexler slipped the knit cap into a plastic bag. "Hand this over for analysis, for one. Then if we pick up Nickels, we have physical evidence."

"I *mean* about picking up Nickels and his partner," Neil clarified. His agitation showing, he was pacing the length of the room. "I *mean* about the attacks on Annabeth. What are you going to do to protect her? Are you going to have a guard at the rodeo tonight in case Nickels shows?"

Neil had told them about his latest vision, though

of course he could not be certain that Nickels would show tonight.

"Like I suggested before," Detective Wexler said, turning his attention to her directly. "It might be best if you stay away from the rodeo for a few days, maybe move in temporarily with a relative or a friend."

"Great idea if only that were possible," Annabeth said. "Like I said, I can't afford to give up work. And I don't have anyone I can impose on."

Detective Smith suggested, "A motel, then."

"And the city would pay?" she asked, knowing what the answer would be.

Wexler muttered something about the tight budget and how they didn't have the funds to guard her.

"You mean you're not going to do anything?" Neil demanded, his voice rising in hearty indignation.

"I can have a squad car come around, keep an eye on this place."

"How often would that be?"

"A few times a shift."

"And what about between those times?"

Detective Wexler raised his arms in a gesture of helplessness.

"I just love the interpretation of justice," Neil muttered. "When you get the bastard, you'll damn well protect *him*—"

"Neil." Annabeth's soft plea added to physical contact as she touched his arm to calm him down. "We'll watch each others' backs. We'll manage."

Her speech was braver than she was feeling, of

course. Her heart was pounding and her stomach tying itself into a big fat knot.

Neil nodded his agreement but didn't give over altogether. "About the search for Nickels and his cohort?" he asked the two cops.

"We'll be on it," Detective Wexler promised.

Detective Smith added, "We can have the Bucktown neighborhood checked out without adding the psychic stuff to the report."

Heaven forbid they should be thought foolish, Annabeth thought. It was only her life on the line.

"And what about the rodeo?" Neil demanded.

"We already got a contingent on the grounds," Smith said. "They'll be alerted."

Detective Wexler added, "We'll have men posted near the entrances and exits. And the men inside will keep an extra eye out for the perps, which brings me to the next thing you've got to do. Come back to the area office with us. Work with Officer Nuhn on getting a visual on the Hispanic now that you've seen him. That way, they'll know who they're looking for. As for you, I'll give you two my beeper number. You see either of the perps, you leave me a message."

Neil gave over. "Fine by me."

Relieved, Annabeth slipped her fingers into his hand. "And by me."

His firm grip as he encased her hand in his relieved some of the anxiety. They just had to keep their heads, to keep thinking, to outsmart the bad guys.

For once, she would control her own destiny.

THE TRIP TO the area office was a productive one. Now they had likenesses of both thieves.

Then Neil escorted Annabeth to work, arriving at three, a half hour before the rodeo grounds opened for the day. Even so, he didn't leave her side until someone was with her so that he could be certain that she was safe.

Then he set out to find Lloyd Wainwright.

It took a while, but he finally spotted the man near the far barn that housed the bulls.

The stock contractor was deep in discussion with Peter Telek. While the old Indian was dressed in jeans and cowboy shirt, long braids hung from below his Stetson and a medicine pouch hung from a leather thong around his neck.

Great, Neil thought. *Two birds with one stone.* Everyone who had been involved in the hostage situation should know what was going on.

"It's mighty peculiar if you ask me," Wainwright was saying in a low tone. "Calves. Steer. Now a couple of bulls. Animals don't just up and disappear into thin air."

"Apparently these did," the rodeo official said. "Must have been some snag along the way."

"I'll be looking into it, believe you me," Wainwright promised. "Insurance or no insurance."

Telek pressed a clipboard on the stock contractor. Wainwright merely glanced at the paperwork before signing. Then his back stiffened as if he finally sensed another presence behind him. He whipped around to face Neil.

His expression closed, he nodded. "Farrell, you lookin' for me?"

If Neil didn't know better, he would think Wainwright had some reason to dislike him. "For both of you." He included the rodeo official in his gaze. "Alderman Lujan, too."

Telek said, "Haven't seen him around today."

"I saw Lujan earlier," Wainwright said.

"Where?"

"On the midway. I was gonna talk to him, but he was having a heated discussion with some guy."

"Discussion or argument?"

Wainwright shrugged. "Whatever."

Neil dropped it.

"What's on your mind, Farrell?" the stock contractor asked.

"I have a warning."

"Warning?" Telek echoed, suddenly sounding intense.

"About the thieves. They're after Annabeth." Neil hastily added, "She's all right at the moment, but she was assaulted last night."

"I got the message about Annabeth's wallet," Wainwright said. "Damn shame. That little lady's luck is plain rotten. I should find her and tell her that I'll cut another check for her in the next day or two. Maybe that'll cheer her up." Then he frowned. "You said the thieves are after her, though. I don't get the connection."

"There were two attacks," Neil explained. "Stealing her wallet got them her address. One of them was waiting for her when she got home last night."

"She's all right?"

"Annabeth is just fine. Mad as a hornet, though, and itching to round up the guys herself. We had some luck in that direction and found where at least one of the thieves has been holed up.''

''How?'' Telek asked, his dark eyes narrowing.

Neil wasn't about to repeat his confession about his precognitive gift. He'd gotten enough flack from Wexler and Smith to teach him a lesson.

''Let's call it luck and leave it at that. Anyhow, we've positively linked the attacks back to the thieves. This morning, we brought Detectives Wexler and Smith up to speed on the situation.''

Wainwright muttered something under his breath. But when Neil gave him a curious look, the stock contractor said, ''Poor Annabeth. A damn scary situation for a woman, her being alone and all.''

''Not anymore,'' Neil assured him. ''She's got me now to help her fight her battles.'' Words that would make Annabeth fighting mad, he was certain, but they'd come out of his mouth before he could think. ''I moved in with her to make sure she has someone watching her back.''

''So the authorities are on the lookout for the thieves now, huh?'' Telek mused. He shook his head. ''Not that they—or you—can keep her safe if a man is desperate enough to make sure he gets away with a crime.''

Neil had no argument there. That was his chief worry—that he would be standing right next to Annabeth when one of the villains made his attempt to shut her up permanently.

And that he would be powerless to stop it.

The reason he'd decided to put everyone at alert was that he didn't trust that the police would be enough. But hopefully these men had formed a bond with her from the dangerous hostage situation they had experienced. With multiple pairs of eyes watching for Nickels and Skull, surely Annabeth would be safe.

At least he prayed she would be.

He pulled a couple of folded sheets of paper from where he'd tucked them behind his belt and handed two to each man. He'd made copies of both police sketches.

Wainwright opened them one-handed. "These are likenesses of the two villains?"

"Right. The head honcho in the hostage situation is called Nickels," Neil said. "We don't have a clue as to the Hispanic's name, but he has a really distinctive feature—a tattoo on his forearm, a skull with a rose in its teeth."

"That's him!" Wainwright said, waving the flyer at Neil.

"Who?"

"The guy Lujan was powwowing with earlier."

"You're positive that you saw one of the thieves *here,* on the festival grounds?" Telek asked.

"I may wear glasses, but these old eyes are still reliable."

"Returning back to the scene of the crime... again," Telek muttered. "Nothing between those ears but a lot of balls, that's for sure."

"And what the hell was Alderman Salvatore Lujan doing with one of our thieves?" Neil mused.

"Maybe Lujan recognized the guy," Telek said. "They took him hostage for a while, remember."

"Maybe Lujan got a better look than he told every-one," Neil agreed.

Or maybe...

"I'll be keeping an eye out for these two," Telek muttered.

"Me, as well," Wainwright said.

The assurances made Neil feel a little more at ease. The more sets of eyes looking for the villains, the safer the woman he was learning to care for would be.

Setting off to find a telephone, Neil dug for Wexler's pager number. If Lujan had reported a run-in with one of the thieves, the detective would know about it.

And if he hadn't...

That gave them all something more to think about, Neil decided.

ANNABETH HAD HELPED Jake get the calves down the chutes and into the waiting pen at the back of the arena when Neil caught up to her.

"I have news. Earlier this afternoon, Lloyd Wainwright saw Alderman Lujan arguing with Skull."

"What?"

"He didn't know who the guy was until I showed him the computer images."

"Lord, that means he's here on the grounds," Annabeth said, suddenly feeling shaky inside. She'd intended to set herself up as bait, but the reality of it was that she wasn't as stoic about the possibility as she'd let on. "Maybe Nickels is here, too. If they are—"

"If they are," he interrupted, "we're covered. I left a message on Wexler's pager and asked him to send extra men to keep an eye out."

"That might cost the city money," she said dryly.

"I also suggested that if nothing were done, I might get my cousin Skelly McKenna to talk to some of his media friends about the situation." Neil grinned. "Skelly used to be a big shot in media circles. He had a television newsmagazine show of his own."

"I hope it works."

Neil sobered and asked, "How are you doing? Really."

"A few butterflies," she admitted, scanning the area with a suspicious glare. But no one was paying her any attention. The few men present tended to their own business as they worked around the area. "I'll be all right."

"Just remember, you're not alone. But don't let your guard down, not even for a minute."

"Are you always so bossy?"

One eyebrow arched right up, practically disappearing under the brim of his Stetson. "I do give orders to my ranch hands on a regular basis."

Realizing he was trying to lighten the mood, she came back with, "Hmm. I'll take that as a compliment."

"As well you should," he said with a slow smile that made her toes curl.

Even so, Annabeth sobered. "Neil, we're going to get through this okay, right? I'm not being stupid just by being here?"

"I think you're very brave."

His way of soothing things between them, she guessed. He wasn't really saying what he thought.

"Yeah, right," she muttered, taking a distinct interest in the tips of her boots.

She knew Neil would prefer she took Wexler's advice. Out of sight, out of mind just didn't do it for her.

Neil touched her face as if to reassure her. As he tilted her chin so that she met his gaze—his eyes darkening with something unspoken—his work-roughened fingertips sent a shiver straight through Annabeth.

"Are you ready to ride, cowboy?" she asked, her voice suddenly rough.

"Always."

The way he was looking at her made her think he wasn't talking about his horse. A flush spread from her neck all the way to her sweet spots.

If only they were alone…

"Well, break a leg," she murmured, the showbiz good-luck wish sounding strange on her lips.

"I'd rather have a kiss for luck."

"Have one, then," she said, going up on her toes to brush one against his cheek.

Neil was too quick for her. He flashed his arms around her waist and pulled her close. She couldn't have dodged his mouth if she had wanted to. But, truth was, she didn't want to. She opened to him gladly, greedily accepted him sliding inside and exploring her.

His holding her like this and kissing her banished

for a moment the terror that her life could become. In his arms, she felt safe. Protected. Cherished.

Too bad he didn't know exactly how he made her feel inside.

Too bad a part of her longed for more. A deeper, more intimate exploration. A real connection. The kind of connection a man and woman discovered together when they made love.

But what if she did make love with him? What then?

Neil had said he cared about her. Was that enough?

She wanted a man who not only cared *about* her but cared *for* her. Loved her. A man who would never leave her.

But in a few days Neil Farrell would be returning to South Dakota.

And she reminded him of his sister.

That sour thought was enough to bring Annabeth to her senses. Murmuring his name, she pulled away only to see his hungry expression.

"P-people are staring," she said, taking a step back.

"Who?"

"Well, they could be."

As a matter of fact, she almost felt as if someone was staring at her now. A shiver threading through her despite the late-afternoon heat, Annabeth looked around, but all she saw were workers minding their own business.

"What is it?"

"My imagination playing tricks on me. I hope."

"I hope so, too," Neil murmured.

But she noticed he, too, took a long look around before they slipped inside the arena.

HE WATCHED ANNABETH Caldwell take her place, ready to run the calves through the chute. Right at this very moment, she was gazing around the arena, casting her baby blues over the audience.

Looking for *him*.

"You won't find me there," he murmured.

She was searching in the wrong direction. And The Lone Ranger, her ardent suitor, was too busy watching over her to see past his own nose.

And by the time they figured things out, it would be too late.

Now they both knew too much.

So now they both had to die.

Chapter Twelve

She had that feeling again. That spine-tingling, gut-wrenching feeling that told her she was being watched.

Gasping, Annabeth stopped what she was doing, and leaving a calf at the start of a chute, whipped around to scan the nearby stands.

But her foe was like the air. Invisible. As were the uniformed police she had expected to see.

"The next contestant is Bob Ray Kaiser from Cotesfield, Nebraska."

The announcer's voice jogged her back to the chute. She looked beyond it, to where Neil kept watch, his amber wolf's eyes continually scanning the crowd but always coming back to rest on her.

Always back to her...

Nodding at him, she got down to business.

Annabeth urged the calf forward and waited for the signal. Kaiser nodded to her and she released it. The calf broke from the chute, and the determined cowboy, chomping down on his pigging string, hightailed it after the critter.

She watched as through a fog, and when the announcer claimed Kaiser's time to be a respectable eight seconds flat, she put her hands together for the man and automatically cheered him on.

But her heart wasn't in it.

Annabeth worked by rote, sneaking looks out into the audience whenever she had the chance. Though the menace to her hung heavy, at times threatening to smother her, she never saw the reality of the threat.

No Nickels.

No Skull.

Just the certainty that one of them was out there. Watching. Waiting for his chance at her.

"...Neil Farrell!"

The announcement jogged her to attention. Neil was up, already backing his horse into the roper's box.

Pulse quickening, Annabeth sensed Neil's intensity and wished for him a big, big win. He'd come in second on his first run and had won the competition the night before, though they hadn't known that for sure until they'd arrived on the festival grounds earlier.

Neil Farrell was already a hero in her mind and heart. She just wanted everyone else to recognize the man as such. She wanted the announcer to call out his name with the lowest time, wanted the audience to make the bleachers shake with their clapping and stomping.

Near breathless with wanting, Annabeth moved the calf into position.

Neil shoved the pigging string between his teeth,

then leaned forward over his mount, one hand tightly clutching the looped rope.

That's when Annabeth felt it again—the sizzle along the back of her neck that told her she was being watched. Before she could check to see what was what, Neil gave her the nod that he was ready to go.

But even as she started to release the gate, Annabeth glanced back, her sharp gaze cutting straight into one set of cold gray eyes not more than a dozen yards away.

Nickels was standing in front of the remaining ropers and their mounts.

He flicked a thumb against the tip of a nasty-looking knife, then nodded sideways toward Neil. His mouth grimaced into an imitation of a smile.

He was taunting her...

Then Nickels turned his gaze from her and centered it on Neil's saddle.

The calf shot out of the box.

And she just knew...

"Neil!" she screamed, competing with the rising arena noise. "Don't go!"

But it was too late. The calf had hit its mark and the tie released. And Neil's horse was already plunging at breakneck speed out of the roper's box.

"Neil!" she screamed again, her chest tightening in fear for him.

He sent that loop sailing smoothly over the calf's neck and tied down the other end to his saddle horn. Before his horse could brake, the calf's frantic rush pulled the rope taut.

And then all Annabeth could do was watch in horror as the saddle slipped sideways and separated from the horse. And the man she cared for more than anything in the world flew to the ground, shoulder and headfirst.

''Neil!'' she screamed again as she rushed forward along with the clowns and a couple of mounted cowboys.

For a moment he was lost to sight.

She whipped around, danced backward, looking for Nickels.

Who had, of course, disappeared.

She plunged into the melee, pushing men bigger than she aside in her frantic attempt to get to Neil, who lay still, his eyes closed.

''Neil! Oh my God!''

Sobbing, she flew to her knees and thought she heard a groan beneath the roar of the anxious crowd. And then his lashes flicked and his eyes opened, his immediate wince telling her that he was in pain.

''Neil, don't move,'' she pleaded, ''not until the paramedics check you.''

His forehead pulling into a frown, he muttered, ''Damn, my headache's gonna have a headache.''

He might be hurting, but he was alive and for the moment, that's all she cared about.

NEIL SHOOK OUT two packets of over-the-counter painkillers—double the suggested amount—and downed the pills with a cup of water. He was a lucky, lucky man. Nothing broken. No concussion.

Just a tree-felling headache, a sprained shoulder

that had already been iced and a body that would be as stiff as a telephone pole in the morning.

Something more to which he could look forward, he thought grimly.

Through his examination, Annabeth had sat in one corner of the trailer, appearing pale and scared until he had been pronounced bruised but not broken. She *still* looked as messed up as he was feeling.

Her gaze met his. Her eyes were rounded and suspiciously moist. Her hands were clenched together as if she was trying to get a grip. Literally.

"Next?" he asked her.

"What?" she whispered, her voice hollow as though she was in shock.

Which she probably was, he guessed. One more incident seemed to be one too many for her.

"Maybe our friendly paramedic here should look *you* over before we leave."

The paramedic—a young, rumpled-looking man named Craig—gave him a surprised expression but didn't say anything, just continued cleaning up the area.

Annabeth said, "I'm not the one who got hurt."

"Couldn't prove it by me," Neil said.

"This is no time for levity, Neil," she said, her voice thick with distress. Frowning, she added, "You're hurt and it's my—"

Neil cut her off. "The best medicine in the world for me would be one of your smiles."

This was not Annabeth's fault. Not her bad karma. And he wouldn't let her blame herself as she usually did when things went wrong.

She frowned harder and seemed as if she were trying to keep herself from crying again.

"Oh, yeah," he muttered. "That'll do it for me."

Wincing, Neil slid off the examination table and tried to appear natural. But his shoulder—and his head—weren't cooperating.

"Thanks for the assist," he told Craig.

"That's my job," the paramedic said. "Take care of that shoulder, and if it doesn't feel better in a few days see a doctor, would you?"

"You have my word on it." Neil turned to Annabeth. "C'mon, let's get out of here. I want to check on Cisco and see what happened to my saddle."

"I can tell you." Annabeth popped out of the chair and was at his side in seconds. "Nickels happened. I saw him when I released the calf." She waited until they'd actually left the first-aid trailer to add, "Nickels had that knife you saw in your vision, but he made it clear that he was after you rather than me. I tried to warn you but it was too late. I wasn't his target this time—*you* were."

Neil nodded and cut across the back lot toward the barn where his horse was stabled. "The moment Cisco tore out of the roping box, I knew something wasn't right. The saddle slid around a bit. I just thought I hadn't tightened the cinch enough."

"Nickels was taunting me, Neil. He *wanted* me to know what he'd done to you."

"Sick bastard!" Neil cursed under his breath and sped up, anxious to make certain that Cisco was uninjured. Annabeth had assured him someone was taking care of his horse, but he wanted to see that all was well for himself.

"How did Nickels get past all those policemen who supposedly had a copy of his likeness?"

"Now don't go blaming the police for everything. They don't have some magic crystal ball...nor any kind of precognitive radar."

"And if they did, it wouldn't matter," she muttered. "They would ignore any clues that were planted right under their officious noses."

Neil let it alone. No need to argue. Let her be angry with someone other than herself.

The electronic voice of the announcer coming from the arena indicated the bull riders were up. The rodeo was drawing to a close for the night. Quite some time had passed since his accident, Neil realized.

They arrived at Cisco's barn and Neil was soon relieved of his worry over the horse when he found him chomping on some hay. He checked the big bay over carefully anyway.

"He's sound," Neil said, rubbing the horse's velvet nose and following the white streak all the way up to the sweet spot just between his eyes.

Cisco threw his head away, then brought it back to lip Neil. "Looking for treats, huh? Sorry, boy, I don't have anything for you tonight."

Leaving the stall, he headed for the tack area. One of the cowboys at the arena had told him he'd take care of everything for him, and he'd come through all right. The saddle was there. As was the proof that this had been no accident. The cinch had been cut by a knife nearly all the way through. The calf jerking on the rope tied to the saddle horn had been all it had taken to make that cinch snap.

"Clever for a greenhorn," Neil said.

"I can think of lots of names to call Nickels," Annabeth said with passion. "Clever not being among them."

Neil would have to see about getting the cinch fixed first thing in the morning if he wanted to continue in the competition. Which he did.

"Now the question is...do I bother making out yet another police report?"

"For all the good it'll do."

"Then Wexler it is. Maybe I can even get him in person this time. I already left him a message about Skull being seen with Alderman Lujan."

"And he didn't get back to you?"

"Considering I don't have a cell phone and that I was on the move," Neil said reasonably, "I don't see how he could have."

They stopped at the barn office. Neil used the phone to leave another message and the number there, saying they would wait for fifteen minutes before leaving for Annabeth's. He left her home number, too.

He'd just set down the receiver when Lloyd Wainwright walked in.

Appearing surprised to see them, the stock contractor said, "You're all right, then." He turned to a back shelf to sort through the phone books.

"Not quite fit as a fiddle, but I don't have one foot in the grave, either."

"What?"

"Nickels tried to kill him!" Annabeth nearly shouted.

"And he did it from the warm-up area," Neil added. "Got to my saddle and fixed the cinch right up."

"He got past me?" Wainwright thundered.

"What did you think happened?"

"I thought you had a dumb-luck accident." Wainwright shook his head. "So the bastard was there tonight, was he?" He picked up a big phone book in his left hand, then almost dropped it before setting it down next to the telephone. "Damn!"

"Something wrong with your hand, Lloyd?" Annabeth asked.

"Just twisted something in my arm working with an ornery bull."

"Maybe *you* should see the paramedics."

"Nah, I ain't no sissy-boy. Not that you are, Farrell," he added quickly. "You really scared the lot of us with that fall you took."

"I'll live," Neil said dryly. "I can't get over the nerve of the thieves, showing up on the rodeo grounds like they did. And Skull with Lujan—"

"Skull?"

"That's what we've been calling the Hispanic thief," Annabeth said. "Because of the tattoo."

"You haven't talked to Wexler or Smith, have you?" Neil asked the stock contractor.

"Not a word."

"Seems to me one of us would have heard if Lujan had reported seeing Skull."

"What are you getting at?"

"I've been wondering how the thieves ever knew about the rodeo bank in the first place."

"You think Lujan..."

Neil shrugged. "He *is* an insider."

"Yeah, but the thieves roughed him up pretty good," Wainwright said in the alderman's defense. "There was no love lost between them."

"But they just set him free later, without really hurting him," Annabeth countered. "That's something to consider."

"And now Lujan is spotted with Skull." The more Neil thought about it the more it made sense that there had been an inside man. "Their being so cocky is going to be their downfall. Sooner or later—hopefully, sooner—someone's going to catch them. Then the jig will be up."

"Yeah," Wainwright agreed. "The jig will be up for everyone involved."

NEIL WAS BEING a real hero, as usual, Annabeth thought, no matter how much he might deny it. He'd downplayed his injury, but now, as he got out of the truck, she could see that he'd already stiffened up.

And by the time they got inside her apartment, he wasn't moving much easier.

"I think you should get in a hot shower and plant yourself there until those muscles feel better."

"Sounds like a fine idea."

And he wasn't sleeping on the floor tonight, Annabeth thought, not when he was battered and bruised on her account. Not that she said so lest she start an argument before she could come up with a convincing plan.

The moment she heard the shower start, she began removing pillows from the couch. Neil deserved a little tender loving care tonight and she was going to see that he got it. He'd been looking after her so closely, and now it was payback time. He needed her.

Did he really need her? she wondered.

Everyone needed someone. She'd been denying that, but now she could admit that she'd been wrong. Being with Neil these past few days had taught her to count on someone other than herself.

And Annabeth wanted Neil to learn the same lesson.

After opening the sofa bed, she changed the linens. Then she retrieved a bottle of scented oil and set it on the side table.

Suddenly realizing the shower was off—no more sound of pounding water—she felt a little light-headed.

Rushing around, she turned off all the lights but the floor lamp. No sooner had she adjusted the dimmer so that it shone upward, softly illuminating the ceiling, draping a romantic glow over the room, than the bathroom door opened. Neil slipped out, his face buried in a towel.

That he was nude from the waist up startled her. Her mouth went dry at the thought of touching that skin, running her hands over that fine musculature. He raised his arms, bringing the towel to his wet hair, and his body resculpted itself. She went weak in the knees and pressed her leg against the edge of the mattress to steady herself.

"So, how should we pass the time until we get sleepy? Television?" Neil's voice was muffled as his head was still enveloped in the towel. "Or would you rather play cards?" He let the towel drop and his eyes went wide. "Uh, I guess neither." He raised a dark eyebrow and asked, "What *do* you have in mind?"

"Massage," she croaked out. "I figured you needed one."

"Oh."

Did he really sound disappointed or was that her imagination?

"So how do we do this?" he asked.

"Lie across the bed."

Neil propped a knee on the edge of the mattress. His amber eyes glowed in the dark. "Are you sure you know what you're doing?"

"Yes, of course. I used to work on Mom's back to get her to relax…"

Suddenly she realized he hadn't been asking if she was proficient in the art of massage…just if she was sure.

Sure that she wanted to touch him so intimately?

Sure that she wanted to provoke more than relaxation?

Sure that she wanted to get in over her head?

Annabeth wasn't sure of anything.

"Lie facedown," she said anyway.

Only after Neil had done as she commanded did she have second thoughts. But knowing how much he was hurting—and, whether or not he agreed, it was because of her—she put her own reservations aside. She had to do something to make it up to him.

Hesitating only a second, she climbed onto the bed next to him and straddled his hips. In reaching for the bottle of oil, she had to lean over his back. The tips of her breasts brushed his warm flesh and her nipples instantly responded.

Below her, Neil sucked in his breath.

"I'm not hurting you, am I?"

"Not exactly," he mumbled into the pillow.

Annabeth heard the stress in his voice loud and clear. Well, a massage would do wonders for him. She drizzled oil on her hands, then a bit more across the top of his back. Capping the bottle, she set it on the bed. Then, shaking away the last of her reservations, she got to work.

The pleasure was as much hers as it was his. She loved the sensation as her fingers splayed across his warm flesh. And when he sighed, she sighed with him.

With a light touch, she began working on his sore shoulder muscles. The hot-water shower had lifted some of the tension from the area, and she worked at it until the shoulder felt relaxed.

But surely the rest of his back would hurt, as well, so she might as well continue the massage.

She smoothed the flesh on either side of his spine, working her way, inch by inch, all the way down to his waist. As if she'd hit a trigger point, Neil suddenly turned and flipped over, taking her with him. Somehow she ended up on the bottom and he was on top.

"You didn't like the massage?" she croaked.

"I'd like to return the favor."

Gently, he began massaging her neck muscles, then worked his way down toward her breast.

Annabeth arched into him.

And then the telephone rang.

Scrunching back down into the mattress, she said, "I should get that."

"Let it ring."

He continued to touch her, stroke her, make her want to forget about anything outside this room.

The telephone shrilled its displeasure and she caved.

"But it might be important."

"It's probably a telemarketer."

"After 10:00 p.m.?"

"Some of them have no sense of decency."

Then her answering machine went on. *Annabeth is busy right now, but she'll return your call as soon as possible. Leave a message at the beep.*

"Miss Caldwell, Detective Wexler here..."

"Omigod!"

Annabeth practically pushed Neil off her and flew for the phone.

"...we've found the man you call Skull..."

"Yes, hello?" she gasped. "This is Annabeth. You say you found him."

"We did, but..."

"But?" She looked over at Neil, who was rising off the bed. "What's wrong? He isn't talking?"

"He can't, Miss Caldwell. He's dead."

Chapter Thirteen

"So what do you really think happened?" Neil asked Detective Wexler early the next morning when the policeman stopped by Annabeth's apartment to fill them in on the thief's death.

"The way I figure it, Estaban Vega and his pal Nickels weren't really as thick as thieves." Seated in the chair opposite the couch, Wexler barked a laugh at his own bad joke. "It's more than likely that Nickels stabbed him in the back to cover his own tracks."

"Who found him?"

"A festival worker cleaning up the place. He went to the Dumpsters behind the midway to throw in a bag of garbage. When he opened the lid, an arm popped out and smacked him on the head."

A picture Neil was not likely to forget. "Why do you assume Nickels is the guilty one?" he asked.

"Who else do I have?"

"Maybe you should talk to Alderman Salvador Lujan," Annabeth said, coming out of the kitchen area to hand the detective a mug of fresh coffee. "Find out exactly what he and Vega were fighting about."

Being that Neil had informed Wexler about Lloyd

Wainwright's witnessing the argument between Lujan and Vega, he was disappointed that the detective hadn't come to that conclusion himself.

Wexler took a long sip of coffee. "Alderman Lujan presents a delicate situation."

"Politics and the law working hand in hand?" Neil asked, raising an eyebrow at the detective.

"C'mon, Farrell, be reasonable. Lujan may not be a pussycat personality-wise, but he is an upstanding member of the community. Before we go around casting aspersions on his character, we have to be sure we got something worth tipping the boat over for."

"And talking to him would tip the boat?" Neil mused. "Asking him about something that happened in a public place would cast an aspersion on his character? Sounds like you think he has something to hide."

"I didn't say I wouldn't talk to him, but I'm going to do it *my* way," Wexler said with emphasis. "Carefully. And I'm not jumping to any conclusions."

Considering the circumstances, Neil figured that was about all they could expect.

Before he could say so, Wexler added, "So don't go threatening me with your cousin again."

"Skelly is a wild card," Neil said, enjoying Wexler's perturbed expression. "He has a mind of his own. Once he has a lock on a situation…"

He took a slug of coffee so he didn't have to finish.

Neil hadn't even spoken to Skelly since he'd made the threat to open the situation to the press. But he did know his cousin well enough. Skelly could be counted on for backup, especially where a family member was involved.

"Detective Wexler, why didn't you just tell us everything over the telephone?" Annabeth asked.

She stood on the other side of the coffee table, obviously too nervous to sit and relax. Her anxious gaze was pinned to the detective.

"I wanted to see you in person, Miss Caldwell," he said, "so I could give you this."

He reached up to hand her something small and black.

"A cell phone?" she murmured.

"Inasmuch as you won't stay away from the rodeo or move out of this place temporarily..." Wexler shrugged. "Consider it a loan. If you see anything, hear anything, smell anything suspicious, I want you to call me. Hit *one* and then *yes* and that'll put you through to my cell phone. And just in case you can't get me there, *two* and *yes* will get you to the area office. Tell the dispatcher I said to put you through to me, wherever I am."

Staring down at the phone in her hand, Annabeth licked her lips, reminding Neil of a nervous cat. He wondered if it was a Chicago Police Department policy to lend cell phones to people in trouble. He suspected not. To Neil's thinking, that showed Wexler to be a decent human being and he regretted threatening the detective with his cousin's media influence.

"Why?" Annabeth asked, her voice suddenly hoarse. "You think I'm in that much immediate danger?"

"What do you think, Miss Caldwell?"

Neil caught Annabeth's expression before she quickly hid her consternation.

"Th-thank you. I won't go anywhere without it," she promised, slipping it into her pants pocket. "At least it makes me feel a little safer."

"Good." Wexler rose as if to go. "Good."

Neil said, "About Lujan—"

"Let me handle that my way. I'll let you know if there's anything to tell."

Wexler left a wake of uneasiness behind him, exactly as he had when he'd called the night before, Neil thought.

Then the mood that had been building between him and Annabeth had quickly dissipated and they'd gone to bed without so much as speaking of what had almost happened.

Annabeth had insisted he take the bed.

Neil had held out for a compromise that had greatly affected his ability to sleep.

They'd shared.

And Neil had been too aware of Annabeth clinging to the edge of the mattress on her side for all she was worth. Obviously she already had regrets.

Unfortunately, this morning she still seemed to be clinging to something intangible, some invisible barrier that she'd erected between them.

"I'm scheduled in early today," she said, removing the coffee mugs to the kitchen.

"No problem."

"No, not for me," she called from the other room. "I need to work. You don't."

"I don't mind spending the day on the grounds."

"I mind."

She stood in the doorway, her arms crossed in front of her. Color was rising in her cheeks to compete with the brilliant rose T-shirt she wore this morning. Her hair was swept to one side and hung over her shoulder, the silken blond strands tempting him even now.

Until she said, "I need some time alone, Neil. I need some time to think."

What did she need to think about? He wondered, the mood broken.

Them?

Him?

She was all he thought about.

"I just want to see that you're safe."

"I am. I have a cell phone now, remember."

Disliking the way this conversation was going— next thing he knew, she'd say she didn't need him at all—Neil said, "A phone won't exactly keep Nickels away from you."

"Neil, please, I need some space."

"And I'll give it to you...after I see you to work," he insisted. "I need to go in anyway, so I can get the cinch on my saddle fixed, remember."

Apparently she realized arguing was useless because she nodded. "Fine."

But the tension wiring between them was negative this time. Neil could tell that Annabeth was freaked out and trying not to show it. So he'd give her that time she needed—a few hours anyway—and then...

Then what?

Exactly the question he hoped Skelly could answer when he showed up at his cousin's house in time for lunch. Roz had taken the kids out for the day, so the town house was abnormally quiet. Oddly, Neil missed the thunder of little feet and the shrill of tiny voices.

Even more odd, he was starting to wonder when he would have kids of his own.

"So, you're still fighting it?" Skelly asked as he plopped bread for sandwiches on a couple of plates.

He didn't have to elaborate. Neil knew Skelly meant their grandmother's legacy.

He knew his cousin meant Annabeth.

"She's not right for me."

"You don't sound convinced," Skelly said. He dug in the refrigerator and came out with a packet of roast beef and some cheese. "Are you sure that you don't mean that Miss Annabeth isn't the woman you imagined you would love?"

Love.

Did he?

Is that what gave him this sick feeling in the pit of his stomach every time he imagined Nickels after Annabeth?

Leaning his elbows on the breakfast bar where Skelly began building them sandwiches, Neil finally said, "Maybe you're right."

"Maybe you thought you would get some nice quiet woman, one who holds the same opinions you do?"

"Well…"

Skelly laughed. And kept laughing long enough to aggravate Neil.

"I don't see what's so funny."

"Do you think there's a man alive who doesn't

have some image of the perfect woman, the one who will fit neatly into his world?'' Skelly asked. He went back into the fridge and retrieved a ripe beefsteak tomato. ''Love isn't neat, cuz, but it sure is interesting. It sure as hell makes it worthwhile to get up in the morning. You'll always be looking around the corner, wondering what's next.''

''That's what I'm afraid of.''

To which Skelly responded with more laughter. But then he sobered and asked, ''Do you regret knowing Miss Annabeth?''

''No, of course not.''

''Does she make your blood sizzle?''

Neil coughed. ''Uh, I—''

''Enough said.'' Skelly cut the tomato and added thick slices to their sandwiches. ''How about…can you imagine living your life without her?''

''It's the living *with* her that worries me.''

Skelly plopped a towering sandwich in front of him. ''You're a McKenna, all right.''

''What's that supposed to mean?''

''That someone has to slap you up the side of your head to get it on straight, to make you realize what's important in life and what's not. So consider yourself slapped. Open yourself up to the possibilities, cuz. Trust dear loving Moira. She hasn't been wrong yet.''

Trust dear loving Moira…

Trust the woman who had passed on to him her gift and her sense of justice, and most of all, her insight. His grandmother seemed to know better than he whom he needed.

Now if only he could trust that part of the legacy to not let him down.

ALL DAY, Annabeth kept touching her pocket to make sure the cell phone was still there. Its bulk comforted her. Help was only two push buttons away.

But while she kept up her guard as she worked, she saw no sign of Nickels. Not in the barns and not on the grounds.

And, thankfully, not in the arena.

She was especially vigilant when the calf roping started, but if he was around, Nickels never showed his face. Paranoid, determined to see past any disguise, she stared hard at every unfamiliar cowboy.

Neil's time was good enough to bring him in second again, this time behind Bill Hamilton. Grant and Hamilton and Neil held the top three cumulative scores with only four-tenths of a second separating third from first place.

Later, after she and Jake had moved the calves back into the barn, Annabeth got that feeling again, the one she'd had the night before. Locking the pen, she slipped her hand into her pocket and curled her fingers around the comfort of the cell phone.

Then, whipping around, she came face-to-face with Salvador Lujan, who stood just inside the barn doors. As usual, the alderman was scowling at her.

"I suppose I have you to thank."

Blood pulsed through her throat as she lightly asked, "For what?"

"For setting the authorities on me about the rodeo bank robbery."

Which meant Detective Wexler had been true to his word when he'd promised to question the alderman, Annabeth realized. "If you have nothing to be guilty over, then you have nothing to fear, right?"

She answered the question without lying but also without admitting that she'd urged the detective to investigate him.

"I've done nothing wrong!" Lujan said in an explosion of spittle that made one of the calves so nervous it complained loudly and squeezed through its mates to the back of the pen. "Supposedly I was fighting with one of the thieves—a man who is now dead—and Wexler wanted to know why I hadn't reported encountering him myself."

Annabeth fought the fear that threatened to choke her, surreptitiously slipped the cell phone from her pocket and held her ground.

"Why didn't you report the incident?" she asked.

"Because it isn't true! I never set eyes on the bastard. And now I'm a suspect in his death."

Lujan presented the perfect picture of moral outrage. Could he be telling the truth? Or at least his version of the truth? Annabeth shifted uncomfortably.

"So you didn't have an argument with anyone yesterday?" she asked.

"I had a heated discussion, all right," he admitted, "but the man was a constituent who recognized me and was giving me a hard time about the trash not being picked up in the ward on schedule!"

"Not Estaban Vega?"

"He told me his name is Hector Sanchez." Lujan

stepped closer. "But interesting that you know the thief's name."

Annabeth had a death grip on the phone but wondered if she'd even have a chance to use it if necessary. "Detective Wexler told me the thief's name just as he did you."

Advancing on her, Lujan shook his head. "When I'm through with you, you'll be sorry you ever crossed me!"

Annabeth's pulse jumped and she blindly felt for the number *one* on the phone. But before she could hit the *yes* button, Neil suddenly appeared on the scene.

"Is there a problem here?" he asked, stepping up to her side.

His wolf eyes flashed in the low light of the barn as he challenged the alderman. And Annabeth's heart thudded harder.

Lujan sized Neil up as though he might take the man on. But in the end, he merely said, "I was just leaving," and then scowled mightily as he passed her.

"What was going on here?"

"Apparently Detective Wexler had that chat with Lujan, who correctly assumed I was responsible for Wexler's questioning him." Annabeth disarmed the phone and slipped it back into her pocket. "He denied the encounter ever happened, though. He admitted to having a heated discussion, as he called it, but with a man who was an unhappy constituent."

"Do you think he was telling the truth?"

Annabeth shrugged. "He was angry but he would be anyway if he were lying. Maybe he didn't realize it was Vega and made up the name to cover. Or maybe Lloyd was mistaken. The computer image is a good tool, but it's not the same as a photograph. And how close was Lloyd to them, anyway?"

"Don't know. It'll be interesting to get Wexler's take on the situation, though." Neil stared off into the distance as if following Lujan's movements. He asked, "Are you done for the night?"

"Almost. Maybe another fifteen minutes."

"You finish up here, then, and I'll wait in the truck. I already pulled in closer, in the vendor area. Meet me there as soon as you're done."

"Fine."

Annabeth didn't bother arguing. As conflicted as she was about their confusing relationships, she felt safest in Neil's company.

That said a lot about her trust in him.

Too bad she had to analyze everything to death.

Too bad she couldn't just go with the flow, let things happen as they would.

Too bad she was in love with a man who wouldn't even be in her life a week from now.

Love.

That had to be it. No other explanation for that crazy roller coaster of feelings that kept assaulting her.

Yes…no…

Hot…cold…

Heaven…hell…

Was that how love was supposed to be?

Why had no one ever told her?

DUSK SETTLED OVER the festival grounds as Neil arrived back at the vendor parking area. At first he thought he was mistaken about where exactly he'd parked the car. Then he realized it was gone.

Towed?

"Damn!"

Some ever-vigilant cop must have noticed he didn't have the official vendor card in his front window. Great. He already had two parking tickets to pay—he'd found the second one that Annabeth had stuffed in the glove compartment. Now this.

Jamming his Stetson down on his head, Neil stormed back toward the barn area to find Annabeth and tell her the good news, when he saw her approaching him. His announcement didn't seem to come as much of a surprise, though.

"You'll probably have to make a bunch of calls to find out where your truck was towed," she said with a sigh. "It'll be easier to do that at my place. Then we can rescue it in the morning."

"We have to get to your place first."

She was already moving off. "Ever hear of public transportation?"

"What about a taxi?"

"When we can get a train that stops a block from home?"

Neil resigned himself.

Annabeth claimed the ten-minute walk to a Loop elevated station would do him good, simmer him down. And who was he to argue?

Festival-goers were leaving the grounds in droves. Surrounded, Neil felt a sense of growing unease. He glanced around but saw nothing—no one—to give him pause. He just wasn't used to such crowds and would be glad when they were out of this mess.

They passed the underground parking entrances and crossed Michigan Avenue, but the human herd surrounding them didn't seem to lessen.

"Not too many people brought cars," Annabeth said. "I have a feeling this is going to take us longer than I expected."

"It's not too late to change your mind about that taxi," Neil said hopefully.

But Annabeth kept going.

They arrived at the elevated structure in a horde of people anxious to get home. Luckily, most already had round-trip fare cards or passes, so the wait at the fare-card machine wasn't too long. Neil put in enough money for one and handed the card to Annabeth. But when he deposited change for his own fare, the machine kept returning his money.

"Must be out of cards," the guy in back of him muttered in disgust. "Damn! Now we gotta wait in line all over again!"

Planning to tell Annabeth what had happened, Neil turned only to realize that she had disappeared.

SHOVED TO the turnstile by the crowd, Annabeth decided to go through and wait for Neil on the other side. Overhead, a train left the station.

Clack-clack...clack-clack...clack-clack...

When she turned back, Neil wasn't at the fare-card machine where she'd left him. And he wasn't in line at any of the turnstiles, either.

"Looking for someone?"

Her blood froze. She'd recognize that voice in her sleep.

Ba-bump...ba-bump...ba-bump...

Heart thundering as fast as the train overhead, she slowly turned to face a pair of cold gray eyes set in a familiar narrow, scarred face.

Nickels!

Frantic, Annabeth turned toward the exit, but Nickels clamped a hand around her upper arm.

"We're going for a little ride."

"I'm not going anywhere—"

"And if you scream and alert anyone," he growled, now close to her ear, "I'll have to kill someone else."

The station was loaded with women and children.

The woman will be the first to die...

Knowing he would do it—that he would kill an innocent to prove a point—Annabeth caved and let Nickels drag her toward the stairs to the train.

"Annabeth!"

Halfway up, she glanced over her shoulder to see Neil coming through a turnstile. Just as he caught sight of them and started pushing through the crowd, Nickels jerked her forward so that she tripped and went down on a step.

"No, you don't," he muttered, hauling her upward.

Annabeth got to her feet somehow and raced up the stairs. The platform was already jammed with people waiting for the next train.

And Annabeth was thinking fast.

Even as Nickels jostled her through the crowd and

headed down the platform, she slipped her free hand in her pocket and turned on the cell phone and lightly touched the pad to find the right buttons.

One.

Yes.

Seconds later, she swore she heard a faint voice coming from her pocket and surreptitiously slipped the unit free.

"Where are you taking me, Nickels?" she yelled over the crowd noise, praying that Wexler, indeed, had answered and that he could hear.

"You're going on a ride straight to heaven."

"You're going to kill me like you did Vega?"

"Vega is dead?" Nickels seemed thrown by that.

And Annabeth took advantage of his hesitation. "On the Brown Line?" she went on. "Couldn't you pick a better place than the new Jackson station?"

Suddenly suspicious, Nickels jerked her around. "What the hell are you doing?" His gaze traveled down the length of her free arm to her hand. "Give me that!"

They wrestled for a moment, but in the end, Nickels wrenched the cell phone from her and threw it over the platform. A spark shot up when it hit the live rail, and then the unit, no doubt dead now, Annabeth thought with regret, bounced off to the side.

The struggle had taken only a moment, but it was long enough for Neil to close the distance between them. Nickels set off, dragging her up another set of stairs to a bridge that connected the two sides of the station.

Annabeth did the only thing she could think of to

slow him down. Three-quarters of the way up, she dropped to the stairs and sat.

Even as Nickels said, "You asked for this," Neil was running up the stairs after them, then leaping over her to get to Nickels.

Both men flew onto the bridge, Nickels backward. Neil went after him.

"Neil, be careful!" she cried as she shot to her feet.

The two were trading blows. She winced when Neil took a hard one to the chin. But he returned as good as he got.

Below, obviously noticing what was going on, people were pointing and shouting.

Ding-ding…ding-ding…ding-ding…

The clang of the bell below was meant to alert passengers to the arrival of another train.

Annabeth saw it rounding the turn as a direct hit knocked Nickels backward, against the bridge railing. Nickels went low and his shoulder caught Neil in the gut. Neil went down hard, seemingly too out of breath to rise.

"Neil!" she cried, her heart lurching when a *click* shifted her gaze to the evil-looking knife that Nickels brandished.

The eerie scenario cast in green light was unreal: Nickels over Neil…knife raising for a strike.

All the fury simmering in her over too many losses came to the fore. She wouldn't lose someone else she loved, Annabeth vowed as she charged Nickels for all she was worth. He sensed her approach too late and turned awkwardly as she came at him, hands out, striking him in the chest with all her considerable strength.

Flailing for balance, Nickels dropped the knife, and from the deck, Neil kicked out and caught him in the back of the knees. Nickels's legs buckled and he fell forward and did a lumbering nosedive straight over the side.

People screamed.

Gasping, Annabeth looked down as the thief and would-be murderer's arm hit the third rail, which sparked and gave Nickels an extra jolt as the momentum of his body flipped him over, facedown, still on the tracks.

Neil made it to his feet and pulled her into his arms, but a horrified Annabeth couldn't pull her gaze free as the train, horn honking, came straight for Nickels.

With an ear-piercing shriek and a shower of sparks, the train slowed and stopped mere inches from the unconscious man.

Chapter Fourteen

Sirens screamed below from the street as a dozen uniformed policemen broke through the crowd. Neil could barely hear their shouts.

"Get back!"

"Emergency!"

"Move! Move!"

Before his amazed eyes, the crowd was shoved back from the platform's edge and one cop jumped down to the tracks to check on Nickels, who lay unmoving.

Annabeth clung to him as if she could no longer stand on her own two legs. She turned her face from the scene and pressed her forehead into the crook of his neck. He felt her trembling against him.

"It's all right," he whispered into her hair. "You're alive. I'm alive—"

"But Nickels isn't."

"I wouldn't be too sure about that."

Below, the paramedics had already arrived. They rolled Nickels over onto a stretcher between tracks and checked his vitals. Neil figured no more than five minutes had passed, so the man had a chance to be revived even if he was technically dead. The electric shock could have done that to him, he knew, by disturbing the rhythm of his heart.

Uniformed men passed equipment down and the paramedics worked over the inert man.

To Neil's continued amazement, the world around them had stopped for a slice of time. Trains were held up from both directions, passengers held back, while a medic hooked a thief and potential killer to lifesaving equipment.

And closer at hand, a uniformed officer was taking the stairs two at a time.

"Come with me!" he barked.

Neil hung on to Annabeth as though she were fragile, even though he knew otherwise. She was strong and possibly the bravest woman he'd ever met. But even so, he could tell she'd come to the end of her line, at least for the moment.

He wasn't at his best himself. Compared to this, life on the ranch was a piece of cake.

The officer was escorting them along the platform, when Annabeth grabbed Neil hard. He saw that she was looking down at the tracks.

"Back!" the paramedic yelled before applying paddles to the downed man's chest.

Nickels's body jerked as it had upon hitting the third rail, and Annabeth made a strangled sound at the back of her throat as if she was about to throw up.

Thankfully, several more uniformed cops opened a path and they were led into a small station office where Detective Dan Wexler waited.

"Clever woman, using the cell phone to alert me," Wexler said to Annabeth. "Are you sure you don't want to join the force?"

"If I ever even hear about a robbery or hostage situation or a mugging, it will be too soon," she said, finally extricating herself from Neil's grasp. "As for the cell phone...I'm afraid it's history. Once I get my rent paid, I'll pay you back, I promise."

Wexler waved the suggestion away. "I'm just happy you're alive."

"Which Nickels may not be," Annabeth said again, voice ripe with worry. "What happens now?"

Wexler whipped out his notebook. "Now you tell me exactly what happened and don't leave anything out."

They'd barely begun when his cell phone rang and he set the notebook down to answer.

"Wexler here." After listening for a moment, he said, "Thanks." He looked from Neil to Annabeth. "They got him. Nickels is alive."

"Thank God," Annabeth whispered.

"And when he wakes up, I suspect he'll be ready to make a deal. If Salvador Lujan was the brains behind the robbery, we'll squeeze it out of Nickels."

And in the meantime, Neil realized, they weren't clear of danger yet.

"THANK GOD HE'S not dead," Annabeth said for at least the tenth time as they finally got back to her place.

They hadn't beaten dawn by much, Neil realized. It was nearly four in the morning and he was exhausted. He couldn't even imagine what she must be feeling.

"It's over," he said, knowing that was an exaggeration. "You saved the day. You're a heroine."

Her expression serious as she gazed into his eyes, Annabeth whispered, "I was desperate, Neil. I was afraid I was going to lose you."

He brushed wisps of hair from her cheek. "And you did what you had to."

As had he. Kicking Nickels when he was off balance had almost plunged the thief to his death, something Neil didn't want to think about. But he didn't have to, thanks to quick work—both Wexler's and the paramedics'.

Kevin "Nickels" Anderson would live another day to go to trial. Once they got his real name, Wexler had run a check on him and learned that the bastard had a rap sheet that went back more than a decade— mostly petty thefts and assault. No surprise to any of them.

Nickels had still been unconscious when he'd been carried off the tracks on a stretcher, so no one knew exactly when he would be in shape to talk.

"This feels weird, not having anything to worry about, no reason to look over my shoulder," Annabeth said. "Is it really over?"

Neil took her in his arms and stroked the fine hair now loose around her shoulders, but still she seemed tense. He rubbed his mouth against her forehead and murmured, "What's wrong?"

"Just thinking. I can't seem to stop. I was remembering how surprised Nickels seemed that Vega was dead.''

"Maybe he didn't kill Vega."

"Then who? Lujan?"

"Wexler promised to take care of it."

"He can question Lujan again all he wants," she went on, "but without proof…"

"He'll get it."

"And if he doesn't? What if Lujan comes after us himself? He's threatened me enough times."

"Wexler's a good cop," Neil reminded her. "He thinks he can make a deal with Nickels. He's come through for us and I trust him to keep his word. So, can we not worry about the alderman for tonight?"

Annabeth nodded and said, "Tonight? It's already morning, you know."

"An even better reason to loosen up or we won't get any sleep."

"Sleep?" she murmured. "Is that what you want?"

With Annabeth in his arms, sleep was the last thing on Neil's mind. Now that she was safe, a weight had been lifted from his soul. He wanted to celebrate. He had enough reasons. Her coming out of this thing unharmed. His love for her. His Grandmother Moira's hopes for him come true.

At last, he believed in The McKenna Legacy.

The powerful connection he'd felt every time that he'd touched Annabeth should have convinced him. Skelly and the rest of his family had been right all along.

"Well?" Annabeth asked a bit breathlessly. "I'm waiting for an answer."

"All right, then. I'd rather do this."

Neil kissed her.

Gently.

Thoroughly.

Telling her with every beat of his heart how very much she meant to him.

ANNABETH SIGHED and let herself be swept away. Any doubts could wait for another day. She wanted this. Wanted Neil. Thank God he was still alive to be had.

That Nickels had almost killed him had made her face how very deep her feelings for this man ran.

"Make love to me," she whispered.

Love me, her heart silently urged his.

In an instant, Neil was stripping pillows from the couch and tossing them to the floor. But Annabeth was too anxious to wait for a bed to be made up. She launched herself at Neil and together they fell back, the pillows cushioning their fall.

"In a hurry, are you?" he asked, looking up into her face.

Straddling him, she said, "I've been waiting my whole life for you."

Neil grinned and kissed her lightly. Annabeth laughed. She'd forgotten what it was like to laugh like this. To feel happy. To feel loved.

At least she thought Neil loved her.

But if he didn't…she wanted this time with him anyway.

The next kiss plunged her into paradise. The aching, writhing passion of something just out of reach taunted her even as did Neil's hands.

His fingers brushed her breasts, smoothed her waist, trailed down her belly until she was fluid with wanting him. Warmth pooled between her thighs and she undulated against the hard length protected by heavy denim until he groaned and slipped a hand between them.

Annabeth realized that Neil was unfastening his jeans and letting loose his erection.

Sighing into his mouth, she found and stroked his hot flesh as he unzipped her trousers and slid them down to her hips. She broke the kiss and raised herself to remove the garment, but he wouldn't let her move away, merely slid them down her thighs and pulled her back over him.

Startled, Annabeth stared into Neil's face. Tension had hardened it and his eyes glowed with amber depths. He needed her. Now. He couldn't wait.

She didn't want to.

Hot and wet and ready, she mounted him despite their tangle of clothes. She slid down him with agonizing slowness and only hoped he wouldn't come too soon.

They were both breathing hard and Annabeth waited for a moment for their pulses to settle.

Then she began to rock, and he slipped his hands up under her T-shirt. He explored her breasts. Her nipples lengthened and he tugged at them until she felt tension stretch between the turgid flesh there and the wet flesh below.

She raised her hips higher, sank them deeper.

He unhooked her bra and gathered all of her full flesh into his hands.

"Now," he whispered, using a pulsing rhythm on her breasts to urge her on.

Annabeth rode Neil in a fury of passion.

They came together, as she knew they would.

A memory that she would hold close.

Forever.

No matter what followed.

ANNABETH WAS on the midway getting a late lunch/ early dinner the next day when Peter Telek stepped up next to her at the booth that sold all-American fast food and suggested they share a table. Agreeable, she ordered a burger and fries to his slice of stuffed pizza. Then they took their trays to one of the picnic tables under the trees.

A strong breeze whipped over them, bringing fine spray from Buckingham Fountain, which was half a block away. Annabeth closed her eyes for a moment and sighed. A cold front had swept through the city and the weather was summer-beautiful.

She took a bite of her burger.

Munching on his pizza, the old Indian stared at her.

"Did I get mustard on me somewhere?"

He shook his head. "How can you seem so happy when you are so bruised?"

Suddenly self-conscious, Annabeth set down her burger and touched her face. "I didn't realize it showed."

"Sometimes old eyes see through things when

young eyes can't." He took a sip of his soda. "And old ears catch gossip on the wind."

Now she understood. He wasn't being literal. "You heard about last night."

"Only that the last thief was caught, and that you were involved."

"Me and Neil."

"He came after you?"

She nodded. "Nickels—actually, his real name is Kevin Anderson—followed us to the elevated station. He grabbed me and made me go with him, but Neil came after us and stopped him. The fight ended when Nickels fell to the tracks."

Telek seemed strangely intent when he asked, "But he didn't die?"

"No, and as far as I know, he hasn't regained consciousness, either. But when he does...well, hopefully, we'll find out whether or not the thieves had an inside connection."

"I see," he said thoughtfully. "Then it isn't over."

A movement to one side caught her eye and she glanced over to find her boss standing a few feet away. He seemed more serious than usual.

"Lloyd?"

"Annabeth, honey, I was looking for you." He held out an envelope and she noticed that his arm was on the mend. "I wanted to give this to you. I cut you another check like I promised."

Taking it from him, she cried, "Lloyd, I could kiss you!"

"Trying to get me into trouble?" he asked, punching at his glasses.

"Trouble?" she echoed.

"With your boyfriend, there. He's looking for you."

She followed his outstretched arm to find Neil heading their way. Something inside her lit as bright as any fireworks display. Just seeing Neil made her feel good. He stopped right next to her.

"Wainwright. Telek." Then Neil looked at her and murmured, "Hey, Sunshine."

While Neil didn't kiss her, he looked as if he wanted to. Instead, he touched the side of her face to smooth back some hair. A thrill shot through Annabeth.

"Hey," she said softly and patted the bench next to her.

Neil slid in. "I spoke to Wexler."

"Nickels came around?" she asked.

"Afraid not. And Wexler's conversation with Lujan went nowhere. He said he's looking further into the alderman's background."

Telek asked, "What does he hope to find?"

"Some connection to the thieves, I guess. Or maybe just bad publicity—something shady in the alderman's past that he can sink his investigative teeth into. He's convinced more than ever that an insider was involved."

"Maybe when Nickels comes to, he'll finger Lujan," Annabeth said.

"Good thing he didn't die, then." Telek concentrated on his pizza.

The possibility that Nickels could still die put a pall over the conversation, Annabeth noticed.

"It's almost time for me to get going, and I haven't eaten anything," Neil said.

"You can have some of my burger," she offered.

"Thanks, Sunshine, but I'll get my own."

As Neil rose, Lloyd said, "Looks like you have a shot at part of that series purse."

"I hope so. It'll help me pay off these city parking tickets."

"You got your truck back in one piece, then?" Annabeth asked.

"Without a scratch. Just a lighter wallet." Neil looked back to Lloyd. "I understand you were a pretty proficient roper yourself in your day."

"You been looking into my background?" Lloyd asked so quietly that Annabeth looked up.

Neil said, "Just keeping my ears open in the arena, Wainwright. When they get bored, the boys do like to talk."

Lloyd grunted. "It's been a while since I competed, but I can still sit a fast horse as good as the next man."

"I don't doubt you can."

Annabeth wondered if she was imagining it or if Neil and Lloyd disliked each other. She didn't really want to know. She liked her boss and he certainly had come through for her with that replacement paycheck. Now she could repay Neil for the rent money.

He and Telek left the table to get back to work as Neil returned with his food.

The newness of their closer relationship left Annabeth feeling a little awkward, but as usual, Neil put her at ease.

"Skelly drove me to get my truck this morning," Neil told her. "He said to say hi."

"Did he?"

"He likes you. He thinks you're right for me."

"What about you?" she asked lightly. "What do you think?"

"I like you, too."

She'd meant the second part—whether or not she was right for him, but either Neil didn't realize it, or he was ignoring the fact. Though she tried to relax, take things one step at a time, his past comparisons of her to his sister and the disapproval that involved niggled at the back of her mind.

Still, she put on a good face. What did she expect? Overnight commitment because they'd explored their desires for one another? He had a whole other life waiting for him.

After they'd finished their meal, they walked to the back side of the arena together. Even now it was starting to fill with an enthusiastic, noisy audience.

"Wish me luck?" Neil murmured.

"Come here, cowboy."

Annabeth grabbed handfuls of his shirt and pulled him close so that she could show him.

Their kisses had changed somehow. Rather than being charged and hungry, they were more tender. Deeper.

Or maybe she was just being more emotional.

Ending the kiss, she whispered, "For luck."

"I'm starting to think that I'm the luckiest man on earth. With inspiration like that, I don't see how I could lose. Just so you know, I'm dedicating tonight's ride to you.''

"Hmm, if you win, does that mean we split the purse?''

"Only if you sweet-talk me into it later." Neil grinned as he backed off. "And I'll surely enjoy your trying." He took one long look around, saying, "You be careful, Annabeth. Don't let down your guard just yet.''

"Be safe yourself, Neil.''

The exchange lifted Annabeth's mood considerably. While she kept an eye out for Lujan or further trouble, she couldn't help but be lulled into believing that her life had taken a turn for the better.

THE TELEPHONE shrilled Neil awake. Annabeth continued to breathe deeply, continued to sleep, so he quickly rose from the sofa bed and snatched up the receiver by the third ring.

"Hello.''

"Mr. Farrell? Wexler here.''

Neil looked at the kitchen clock. It was already after ten in the morning, but they'd barely slept. Once with Annabeth had not been enough. Neil didn't know if *enough* was possible where she was concerned.

Wiping the sleep from his eyes, he muttered, "What can I do for you, Detective?''

"Nothing at the moment. I, uh, have some bad news and thought you would want to know right away.''

"About Lujan?''

"About our friend Nickels. He died in the early-morning hours without ever regaining consciousness."

Neil's heart sank. He'd been the one who had sent Nickels sailing over the railing to his death. His fault that a man was dead. No matter that Nickels would have killed them both, this would be on his conscience forever.

Sick inside, he asked, "That it?"

"For now. There will be an investigation, but I'm sure everything will work out all right. In the meantime, I have to ask you not to leave town until this is all settled."

"I wasn't planning on going anywhere just yet."

"Good. Good."

Neil hung up, cursing. *An investigation.* He cursed some more.

"What?"

He turned around to see Annabeth sitting up, long blond hair flowing over her naked breasts. She had that look of a woman well loved. Of one who might be in the mood for more. The enticing thought should be enough to set him off again, but it didn't.

"It's Nickels...he's..."

He didn't have to say more. From the way her eyes went round, she understood.

"If only I hadn't let myself get so involved in the first place," Neil muttered, "this never would have happened."

The words were out of his mouth before he could stop them. He regretted killing a man, regretted not letting the police handle it as he'd known he should have. He didn't regret making love to Annabeth. Or loving her, for that matter. But he could see from her horrified expression that she wasn't separating one from the other.

"Annabeth—"

Naked, she stood and walked into the bathroom without saying a word to him.

Not knowing what to do, Neil stared at the door until the shower drummed against his thoughts, effectively obliterating them. At a loss, he picked up his jeans from the floor, pulled them on and made a pot of coffee.

Nearly a half hour later, when Annabeth emerged fully dressed, Neil had downed four cups and worried himself into a state. He decided to try again.

"Annabeth, I didn't mean that the way it sounded."

"No, of course not."

"I just meant maybe we should have figured out a different way, left the investigating to the professionals."

"Right. Maybe that would have been best," she said coolly. In control, she was calm and collected. And sounding bitter. "Then you could have proved your grandmother's legacy wrong."

"No. That—you and me—has nothing to do with it."

"That has everything to do with this, Neil. You wanted out from the first. You're sorry you ever got involved. And I'm sorry I talked you into it."

"Annabeth—"

"I need to get to work."

"Give me fifteen minutes to shower and shave."

Ignoring him, she walked out the door.

"Annabeth, wait!"

She didn't so much as look back.

His gut tying itself into a knot, Neil told himself to calm down. She was angry with him, but she would get over it. When she had time to think things over, she would understand what he meant.

Pacing, he nearly stumbled when his bare foot caught in the T-shirt that he'd stripped from her the night before. Missing her already, Neil swooped down to fetch it.

The moment he inhaled her fragrance, he felt his surroundings fade...

Annabeth's eyes go wide and the breath catches at the back of her throat.

Her fear is palpable, as fierce as the beat of her heart.

Ba-bump...ba-bump...ba-bump...

"*You!*" *she breathes...*

As Neil returned to reality with an unpleasant jolt.

"Where the hell is she? What's going to happen?"

He shook the T-shirt as if it would reveal its secrets, but Neil got no more from the soft material that belonged to the woman he loved.

What the hell was going on?

The vision had been so short it might not have transpired at all. A flash and not a clear one at that, almost like a television program that he couldn't tune in properly.

And then it hit him.

Every other time he'd had a precognitive episode,

Annabeth had been present and they'd had physical contact.

But he hadn't been touching her and she wasn't even close by—so what did his having a vision now mean? Was it merely a progression of his gift? Or an extra–alarm warning?

Fearing to guess at the details, Neil got ready to go after her.

Chapter Fifteen

Annabeth caught a bus to work. After the horror she'd experienced the other night, she was off the El, perhaps for good. The ride might be longer, but it gave her time to think things through.

What was wrong with her? She'd known Neil was going to leave. She'd known she would have to be content with memories. What she hadn't figured on was the regret she'd heard in his words. That he regretted getting mixed up with her hurt more than she might have imagined.

But how could she blame him? A man dead. Something that would haunt them both forever, she expected. Nickels's demise had been a team effort, after all.

She'd managed to put that to the back of her mind by the time she got to work. Work—exactly what she needed. Hauling feed might be physically exhausting, but at least it relieved some of her stress. She needed to be tired enough so that she could sleep at night.

She was doing just that when she realized she wasn't alone. Looking up, she found Neil watching her, and all the disappointment from that morning came tumbling back to weigh down her heart.

"You're all right," he said.

Though he appeared genuinely relieved, she steeled herself against going all soft inside.

"I'm fine, thanks," she said coolly.

"I was worried when you left like you did."

"I didn't want to be late to work, especially not after Lloyd went to the trouble of cutting me another check."

Which, she reminded herself, she still had not cashed.

"You're angry with me and I don't blame you. I could have chosen my words more carefully."

"Why? You meant them."

He shifted uncomfortably. "Yes, but—"

"That's that, then."

"I'm not sorry I got involved with you, Annabeth. I'm just sorry I had to be the one responsible for a man's death."

"I'm equally responsible, Neil. Maybe more. I was the one who wanted to get Nickels. Well, I certainly did that. You never did approve of my wanting to go after him in the first place."

He never approved of *her,* Annabeth thought. And now he was saddled forever with a guilt that was her fault. She had pushed him into action he'd wanted no part of. No matter that he said he didn't regret getting involved with her, he would never be able to forget that.

"Can we get out of here—go someplace else to talk?"

"I'm working, Neil, and talking won't change what happened. And you have to compete in what—an hour or so? You'd better go check in with Cisco."

"Please."

"We have nothing to discuss."

"We have everything to talk about," Neil insisted. "How about later, after work?"

Feeling herself weakening, Annabeth clenched her teeth together and refused to answer.

Neil nodded and backed off, saying, "Later, then."

Alone in the barn once more, Annabeth closed her eyes and whispered, "Good luck, Neil. And I hope you go home the big winner."

ANNABETH WAS SAFE. That was the important thing.

But as Neil left the barn, he wondered for how long. Across the preparation area, he spotted Alderman Salvador Lujan and rodeo committeeman Peter Telek together. Deep in conversation, neither man noticed him.

That Lujan was still walking around free made Neil uneasy. Wondering if Wexler's investigation had turned up anything of significance about the alderman, he checked his watch and decided he had plenty of time to make a phone call before he had to tack up Cisco. He headed for the barn office and phone.

Once there, he dialed Wexler's cell phone. Two rings and the man answered.

"Detective, this is Neil Farrell. I was wondering what you'd dug up on Lujan."

"Sorry to disappoint you, but nothing incriminating yet. Actually, just the opposite. I found Hector Sanchez—the man he claimed he had the disagreement with the other day. Sanchez confirmed it.''

So Lujan hadn't been arguing with the thief. Or had he been?

"How can you be sure Sanchez didn't lie for Lujan?"

"Unless my radar is way off, Sanchez dislikes Lujan for the bigmouthed politician he is.''

"Then why would Wainwright have lied?"

"Maybe he was mistaken. Or maybe Lujan had more than one argument in the same day.''

Neil could certainly believe that. "Thanks, Detective. Keep us posted.''

Thoughtful, he hung up and checked his watch again.

Time to saddle up.

On automatic, he went through the routine, then led Cisco into the waiting area. He didn't stray far from his mount but stood there watching Annabeth's every move as she ran the calves through the chute.

Even sweaty and dusty, she was a beautiful sight to behold, one he didn't want to lose. But when she looked his way, her expression chilled him. It seemed resigned, as if she was trying to tell him goodbye.

And then it was his turn to ride.

Even though Nickels was gone, Neil checked his cinch and tack over for tampering one last time before mounting up.

As he backed into the roping box, he looked over to the chute only to see Jake manning it. Startled, he wondered what had happened to Annabeth. Telling himself not to panic, he looked around but didn't see her anywhere.

A warning in his gut told him he needed to get to her fast.

And so after he gave Jake the nod, he set off after his calf, roped and tied the critter in his fastest time ever.

Then he rode up to Jake. "Where's Annabeth?"

"Said she just needed to get away. She asked me to take over for her."

Neil rode Cisco toward the arena exit, praying he would find Annabeth safe and well.

SHE'D HAD to get away.

Annabeth hadn't wanted to watch Neil ride one more time, not when she might break down crying. So she'd left the chute to Jake and hoped Lloyd would understand and not fire her on the spot. She only had a few days of work left and she needed every hour of pay she could make.

After that, she didn't know what she was going to do. The city had held little charm for her before she herself had been entangled in violence. Now the very idea of staying here was out of the question. She would move, maybe to Lincoln where she had relatives. A mother. That wouldn't mean she'd given up, Annabeth thought fiercely, not the way her mother had.

She entered the barn, which held a surprise—Lloyd himself in a pen with calves.

Certain that she'd never seen these particular calves before, she said, "You found our missing critters."

Lloyd started. "Annabeth, you startled me." He cut through the miniherd toward her. "Yeah, they finally turned up. Better late than never, right?"

"Right."

Wearing one of his fancy shirts, Lloyd had rolled up his sleeves—an attempt to keep them clean, she guessed. But her gaze slipped to his forearm with the wound that had not yet healed.

The wound looked exactly like a bite. Her eyes widened. A human bite?

She remembered biting the man who'd attacked her on her stairs...

The short hairs at the back of her neck stirred and Annabeth lifted her gaze to meet Lloyd's. And in that meeting, she recognized the truth.

"You...you were behind everything!"

His smile faded. "I was afraid you'd figure it out eventually."

"You hired those thugs to rob the rodeo bank?" The breath caught in her throat at the thought that she'd trusted this man. "Why?"

"Business."

"Business? You mean stealing?"

"Stealing...scamming..." He heaved a big sigh. "Whatever you want to call it doesn't matter to me. Been saving for my retirement for years. And now it's time I take it easy. This theft was gonna be my big score. My retirement insurance. And it should have been a breeze with my information and a couple of locals handling it. But you ruined it, Annabeth, when you created havoc in the hostage situation and the money got left behind. *You* ruined it for me," he repeated with emphasis.

Anger and the need for answers competed with a healthy dose of fear that rooted her to the spot. "Is that why you attacked me?"

Rolling down his sleeves, Lloyd shouldered past her to get out of the pen. "I couldn't let you identify Nickels. And I had to take care of him too—a pillow makes a silent weapon. He might have talked to save his own hide."

"So you killed both him and Vega?"

Lloyd shrugged. "They thought they were gonna get money out of me. They were scum."

And he wasn't?

"Why the ruse, Lloyd?" she asked, wanting the whole truth now that she had him cornered. "Why lift my wallet? You had my address on my work application."

"I wanted to throw suspicion elsewhere, of course. If I had just shown up at your place without covering my tracks, Detectives Wexler and Smith might have wondered how Nickels or Vega could have known where you lived. Eventually, they would have looked at me."

"And I suppose you cut me that duplicate check so I wouldn't suspect you."

"Smart girl. I like you, Annabeth, I really do. Too bad I gotta kill you," Lloyd said, slipping a hand into his pocket and pulling out a gun. "And this time, there's no one around to save you."

AT THE BARN DOOR, Neil froze when he heard Wainwright's threat. He slipped into the shadows and cautiously peered inside to see a shaking Annabeth glaring at the stockman, whose back was to Neil.

"I don't need someone to save me," she said. "I'm not afraid of you!"

Neil silently cursed—she was taunting the man. Part of another of her impulsive plans?

Wainwright laughed. "You ought to be afraid."

"You won't get away with this, Lloyd."

"But I will. No one has a reason to suspect *me* here. Why, I was one of the victims."

"So was Alderman Lujan. You made a mistake when you pointed a finger at him."

"C'mon, Annabeth," he said, grabbing her arm and jerking it. "Let's go down to the lake. The fish are waiting."

"How is it the thieves took you hostage, Lloyd? I don't believe that was part of your plan."

"An ugly coincidence." Wainwright's voice hardened. "Now move."

Neil drew farther back into the shadows as Annabeth stepped out of the barn, the stockman right behind her. He could tell from the set of her body that she was winding herself up for a desperate attempt of some kind.

Neil waited only until they cleared the building before launching his attack. He flew at Wainwright from behind at an angle and practically knocked the bigger man off his feet.

"What the hell!" The stockman wheeled around, gun hand first.

That's when Annabeth launched herself at him, knocking his arm upward so that he shot at the stars.

"Annabeth, get out of the way!"

She didn't move fast enough.

Wainwright wrapped a meaty arm around her neck and pointed the muzzle of his gun at her head even as a couple of other people came out to investigate.

"Stay back or I kill her!"

Neil could smell fear on the stockman now, and he knew from experience that a cornered animal was dangerous.

"No use killing Annabeth, Wainwright. Too many witnesses. It's over. Let her go and give yourself up."

"Like hell I will. Move, Farrell, and she dies."

With the gun still to Annabeth's head, he dragged her back and looked around wildly.

Helpless to do anything but watch lest he carry the guilt of being responsible for the death of the woman he loved, Neil connected with Annabeth and concentrated.

Give me a clue, Sunshine.

Neil's reality suddenly shifted...

A determined expression hardens Annabeth's face as Wainwright drags her backward.

She meets Neil's intent gaze and nods, then goes limp...

Neil had difficulty separating the minivision from the reality that tumbled directly on top of it, but the moment Annabeth dropped and took Wainwright off balance, he was after the bastard.

Cursing, the stockman let go of Annabeth and ran toward a cowboy who'd been cooling down his still-saddled horse. He waved the gun, took the reins and then mounted.

One swift look at Annabeth assured Neil that she was all right. "Get a hold of Wexler!" he shouted as he went for Cisco at the water tank.

Wainwright headed the pinto past the arena. By the time Neil was in the saddle, the other man had disappeared from sight. No matter. He aimed Cisco in the same direction, which took him toward the midway crowded with thousands of people.

Wainwright veered around one of the rides and headed straight across the center of the midway, scattering angry pedestrians. Closing the gap, Neil followed suit until a policeman on a bicycle got in the way to stop him.

"What the hell do you think you're doing, cowboy?" the cop asked.

Never taking his eyes off the villain, he said, "Call Detective Dan Wexler and tell him Neil Farrell is trying to stop a murderer, pronto!" He rounded the bicycle and avoided the cop's reach.

He charged off after Wainwright who'd come out on the other side and was now nearing Buckingham Fountain. A cloud of pink dust rose around him as his horse's hooves scattered the fancy fine gravel. People who were oohing and aahing the water display turned to stare after them, and when the stockman turned in his saddle to shoot at Neil, a little kid started screaming.

Luckily, he missed.

"Stop before you hit some innocent bystander!" Neil yelled.

Sense must have knocked into him because Wainwright threw the loaded gun to the ground before he took off at breakneck speed.

A couple of kids went after the weapon, but Neil beat them to it, swooping over his saddle and grabbing the gun before it got in the wrong hands. He stuffed it in his waistband and saw that Wainwright had set off across Columbus Drive and was heading for the city proper.

Following, Neil muttered, "Where the hell do you think you're going?"

Into traffic.

Wainwright charged through a line of cars. Horns blared and his horse jumped to the side and fought him, but the man knew his stuff. He had the pinto back under control in seconds and was dodging him between cars.

Crossing over a bridge, Neil was stopped by traffic. Wainwright had been foolhardy enough to dash through the intersection anyway to the accompaniment of much honking, and the gap between them widened. Ahead, the stockman now passed between two bronze statues of mounted Indians with bows and arrows.

Surreal, Neil thought.

The statues...the cars...the skyscrapers...two horses and riders in the midst of it all.

Make that four.

From the corner of his eye, he saw two uniformed men on horseback picking their way from Columbus Drive between cars. Part of the Chicago Police Department mounted patrol, they were heading straight for him.

When the light changed, Neil charged out through the intersection. Wainwright was caught up ahead in the congestion at Michigan Avenue. A policeman directing traffic was yelling and coming at him.

"Whoa, cowboy!" one of the mounted cops yelled at Neil.

Neil yelled back, "Join the posse!"

"Stop, now!"

Certain he would be able to narrow the gap, Neil ignored the command. Ahead, Wainwright rounded the corner. Spotting Neil, the traffic cop blew his whistle and tried to step in front of him. Neil dodged the cop and went after the stockman, straight down Michigan Avenue.

Surreal, he thought again as he took his looped rope in hand.

More cars...more skyscrapers...two bronze lions observing them from the front steps of the Art Institute.

Neil leaned over Cisco and brought up the rope and whirled it overhead. Then he let loose and the looped rope went sailing, landing square around Wainwright's shoulders. He yanked out the slack and Cisco slid to a stop. Wainwright was jerked off the saddle onto the street, the wind knocked out of him.

Before the stockman could regain his breath, Neil had dismounted and had run the length of rope to the toppled man. He trussed both of Wainwright's hands to one of his feet almost like he would a calf or, more appropriately considering the man's size, a steer. Only he did so behind his back so that he couldn't work himself free.

"What's going on, Mommy?" he heard a kid ask as bystanders cheered.

"It's part of the festival entertainment. If you ask me, it's downright irresponsible!"

Neil shoved a boot under Wainwright's chest and flipped him over to look him in the face.

"Took me a while to rope you," he drawled, "but that might just be my best ride yet."

ANNABETH NEVER STOPPED praying for Neil until he returned to the arena area under the escort of two mounted policemen. The horse Wainwright had confiscated trailed behind them.

The welcome sight lifted a weight from her shoulders...and especially from her heart.

"Thanks for the escort, fellas," Neil said. "I can take it from here."

"You shouldn't have gotten yourself involved at all," one of them replied.

To which Neil most certainly must agree, Annabeth thought, remembering the fierceness of the regret he'd expressed that morning. Though what he was thinking now she couldn't tell—he was staring at her with a strange expression.

Her pulse fluttered as the other cop asked, "Ever heard of 911?"

Neil didn't say a word. Both policemen turned their horses—retired Thoroughbreds, Annabeth knew—and moved off, leaving Neil to dismount.

She worriedly searched him for new signs of injury even as she asked, "Where's Lloyd? He got away?"

She was steeling herself from jumping Neil and smothering him with kisses in her gratitude that he was still alive. He hitched both Cisco and the pinto near the water trough before turning his full attention to her.

"He's in the back of a squad car on his way to the police station now," Neil told her.

She closed her eyes for a moment and offered her silent thanks. "It really is over, then."

"Not exactly. Wexler showed up—he's the one who took Wainwright into custody. We have an appointment with him as soon as we can get there."

And no doubt Neil would have to stick around for a few days past the rodeo closing until the facts of the case were in order. Then she supposed he would return to South Dakota until Wainwright's trial came up.

She said, "We'd better get going, then."

"First we need to get some things straight between us."

The way he was looking at her...

Though she couldn't control her emotions or the way her heart skipped a beat at the *us* reference, she could control what she said to him. "What's the point?"

"The point is that I love you, Annabeth Caldwell," Neil said, making her eyes widen. "No, make that I'm *in love with you*. You are my legacy."

"Your grandmother's wishes mean that much to you?"

"*You* mean that much to me," he insisted, taking her in his arms and ignoring the fact that she was trying her best to resist. "If Wainwright had killed you…"

"Well, thank goodness you outguessed him," she said breathlessly while pushing at his chest to no avail.

His wolf's gaze captured hers and Annabeth went still. He was breaking down her defenses. If she let him, he would break her heart in the end. Who was she kidding? When he left, he would break it no matter what.

"I saw what was going to happen right before you let your weight drop. Twice today I had premonitions, Annabeth, both about you when I wasn't even touching you. So you really have no choice."

Hardly daring to breathe, she echoed, "Choice? About what?"

"About admitting that we were meant to be together. That you love me. That you'll marry me and go back to South Dakota with me."

Even as her heart lifted at his proposal, she argued, "But I'm not right for you, Neil. I'm too strong-headed. Too impulsive, too—"

Neil stopped her protests with a kiss.

For a moment, Annabeth lost herself in the heady sensation of feeling his mouth covering hers. She leaned into him and he hugged her even tighter.

And when he raised his head, he didn't give her room to object. "We are different. That's exactly why you are right for me, Sunshine. Together, we fit like the pieces of a puzzle. You've been missing from my life until now. So marry me and complete me.''

The backs of her eyelids stung with unshed tears—this time of happiness, when Annabeth whispered, ''Yes, Neil, yes.''

Epilogue

Neil chomped down on the pigging string and gave Annabeth the nod.

The calf shot out of the chute. Cisco practically vibrated with excitement until the calf hit the end of his score and Neil signaled him to go.

Loop roiling overhead, Neil leaned over the big bay's neck and spotted his target—bull's-eye!—then yanked the slack out of his rope. Cisco braked to a stop. Neil dismounted, flanked the calf and trussed three of its legs together.

A good run, he thought, throwing up his hands and remounting.

"Neil Farrell…seven-point-one seconds… Ladies and gentlemen, give a big hand to the winner, not only of today's calf-roping event, but of the week-long series!"

Neil sought out Annabeth. She was grinning from ear to ear, lit up from the inside out, truly the sunshine of his life.

The celebration afterward was a family affair at an outdoor restaurant overlooking the lake at Navy Pier. And Annabeth was warmed to her core to be part of it, especially since Neil announced they were to be married.

"Ah, sweet Moira is some matchmaker, is she not, even from the great beyond," Skelly said, hugging his wife, Roz, close.

The triplets had slithered away from them and were playing ring-around-the-dinner-table.

Keelin gave her husband, Tyler, and their daughter, Kelly, a soft look. "Indeed, Gran was a wise, wise woman."

"Hmmph. It's dreadful being the youngest of this branch of McKennas," Alicia grumbled, "wondering what's in store for me and with more than a year to wait." She held up her glass. "But in the meantime, congratulations, Neil and Annabeth."

"Congratulations!"

They all clinked glasses.

Annabeth grinned and leaned into Neil. She seemed to be doing that a lot lately—both the grinning and the leaning.

"Do Aunt Rose and Uncle Charlie know?" Alicia asked.

"I called Mom and Dad this morning. They couldn't be more delighted."

"I almost forgot." Skelly handed Neil an envelope. "This came for you from Rose just today."

"Thanks."

Upon opening it, Neil shook a smaller envelope from the larger one. This one was addressed to him at home in South Dakota, Annabeth noted. Home. She was going to have a new home away from the city.

A ranch wasn't a farm, but it was close enough for her.

"From my brother Quin," Neil muttered, tearing open the envelope and lifting out a single sheet of paper.

Even before he could unfold the missive, he froze.

And Annabeth's stomach did a roll. He'd checked out for the moment and she knew he was having a vision.

As did the entire family, who sat forward in their seats waiting for him to come back to the present.

Suddenly he shook his head and blinked madly, as if trying to focus, then opened the note and quickly scanned it. When he looked up, a wry smile tugged at his lips.

"It's my brother Quin…I saw him laughing at me. He's always had the gift. He writes that he saw the two of us together, exchanging vows." He waved the note. "He can't make it to the wedding, but he says now I can stop being mad at him since I'll have a partner to help me run the ranch."

The McKennas let out a collective breath.

Annabeth smiled dreamily. She was going to have a new home away from the city.

"What are you grinning about?" Neil whispered.

"The future…partner," she said, sealing the deal with a kiss.

Princes...Princesses...
London Castles...New York Mansions...
To live the life of a royal!

**In 2002, Harlequin Books lets you escape to a
world of royalty with these royally themed titles:**

Temptation:
January 2002—*A Prince of a Guy* (#861)
February 2002—*A Noble Pursuit* (#865)

American Romance:
The Carradignes: American Royalty (Editorially linked series)
March 2002—*The Improperly Pregnant Princess* (#913)
April 2002—*The Unlawfully Wedded Princess* (#917)
May 2002—*The Simply Scandalous Princess* (#921)
November 2002—*The Inconveniently Engaged Prince* (#945)

Intrigue:
The Carradignes: A Royal Mystery (Editorially linked series)
June 2002—*The Duke's Covert Mission* (#666)

Chicago Confidential
September 2002—*Prince Under Cover* (#678)

The Crown Affair
October 2002—*Royal Target* (#682)
November 2002—*Royal Ransom* (#686)
December 2002—*Royal Pursuit* (#690)

Harlequin Romance:
June 2002—*His Majesty's Marriage* (#3703)
July 2002—*The Prince's Proposal* (#3709)

Harlequin Presents:
August 2002—*Society Weddings* (#2268)
September 2002—*The Prince's Pleasure* (#2274)

Duets:
September 2002—*Once Upon a Tiara/Henry Ever After* (#83)
October 2002—*Natalia's Story/Andrea's Story* (#85)

**Celebrate a year of royalty with
Harlequin Books!**

Available at your favorite retail outlet.

HARLEQUIN®
Makes any time special ®

Visit us at www.eHarlequin.com

HSROY02

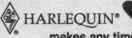

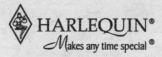

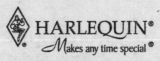